"Are you going to put on a ten-gallon hat, boots and spurs?"

He grinned. He'd been a cowboy for Halloween five years in a row. "I just might, ma'am," he drawled and pretended to tip an invisible hat at her.

"Can I go, too? This I have to see."

His eyebrows rose in surprise. "Are you inviting yourself along?" He had to stop himself from yelling out "yes." *Play it cool,* he told himself.

"I think I am."

His heart raced and his hands started to sweat. "I'm really going to just take photos. Photography is my hobby."

"Really? My brother, Ben, is into photography."

"Then tomorrow's a date."

He couldn't help his next move. She looked so delectable with the evening breeze tugging at her hair and with her face so calm and serene.

He set his wineglass down, pulled her into his arms and kissed her. Her lips were warm and pleasantly sweet with the wine. Her body leaned into his, and he felt every soft curve, smelled her faint perfume, and knew he'd wanted to kiss her since the moment he'd met her at the bar by the pool.

J.M. JEFFRIES

is the collaboration between two women who are life-long romance-aholics. Jacqueline Hamilton grew up believing that life should always have a happy ending. Being a military brat, she has lived in some of the most romantic places in the world. An almost lawyer, Jackie decided to chuck it all, live her dream and become a writer. Miriam Pace grew up believing in fairy tales. She found her Prince Charming and has been married to him for thirty-seven years. Now a granny, Miriam reads fairy tales to her grandchildren and is looking forward to baby Pace, who is due soon.

LOVE'S
Wager

J.M. JEFFRIES

HARLEQUIN® KIMANI™ ROMANCE

Jackie: To all my super baristas old, new and future. Thank you for going on the journey with me, for being there for me and letting me mother you. You make me laugh and you inspire me.

Miriam: To my grandson Frederik, granddaughter Kathyn, and future baby Pace, I wish you the best life has to offer. Follow your dreams.

PLEASE RECYCLE • THIS PRODUCT IS RECYCLABLE

Recycling programs for this product may not exist in your area.

ISBN-13: 978-0-373-86384-6

Love's Wager

Copyright © 2014 by Miriam A. Pace and Jacqueline S. Hamilton

For questions and comments about the quality of this book please contact us at CustomerService@Harlequin.com.

Printed in U.S.A.

HARLEQUIN®
™ www.Harlequin.com

Dear Reader,

One thing we forget is change happens regardless of whether you want it or not. Every time change is on the horizon, we have a decision to make. Do we fight it and preserve the status quo, or do we embrace it and go headlong into a great adventure?

Jackie says change is only good when she wants it. Change is a battle to be waged according to Miriam. For Nina Torres and Scott Hunter, change is a fact of life. Join them as they plow through their unexpected surprises, life-altering decisions and the greatest adventure that awaits them in Reno, Nevada, the biggest little city in the West.

Much love,

Jackie and Miriam

Chapter 1

Holding a glass of her favorite Chardonnay, Nina Torres followed the hostess to her booth. Lua el Sol had been her father's idea. The restaurant featured the best food, music and decor his Brazilian home had to offer.

Lua el Sol was a riot of color with green palm trees at various intervals, fan-backed wicker chairs at the tables and booths along the walls upholstered in bright blue. Huge *carnaval* masks hung on the walls, the brilliantly colored feathers swaying with the air currents. Birdcages dotted the huge restaurant with bright-hued, plush-stuffed parrots inside. Nina's father, Manny Torres, had tried to use real parrots, but they squawked too loud and distracted the diners. He'd donated them to the Los Angeles Zoo and replaced them with stuffed ones.

Nina waved at her mother, Grace Torres, as she slid into the booth. Grace was a beautiful woman with smooth, mahogany-colored skin, masses of black, curly hair tumbling down her back and slanted brown eyes. She was still slender despite having seven children. Nina, the eldest of the only two girls, looked just like her mother except for being several inches taller and slimmer. Her chin-length black hair, more wavy than curly, framed her narrow face and pointed chin. Her eyes were more amber than brown.

Nina loved her parents' restaurant. She loved the boisterous atmosphere as waitstaff maneuvered through the tables, trays piled with an array of enticing, delicious food. The aroma of spice hung heavy over the room.

"Nina, sorry to be late, traffic was horrible." Kenzie Russell dropped her purse on the table and reached out her arms to Nina.

Nina jumped to her feet. "Kenzie, don't worry, I've only been here a few minutes. Hello, Miss E." Nina embraced her best friend and leaned over to kiss Kenzie's grandmother on the cheek. Nina and Kenzie had met their first year at UCLA when they'd roomed together and had been best friends ever since.

Miss E. hugged Nina tightly. She was the grandmother Nina never had, since her father's parents lived in Brazil and her mother's parents had passed away when Nina had been a child.

"Kenzie tells me you won a hotel/casino in a poker game. Good for you." Nina slid back into the booth. Miss E. sat and Kenzie slid in to sit next to Nina.

Kenzie was a gorgeous woman with shoulder-length black hair that she'd pulled up into a French knot at the back of her head. She wore a stylish, blush-pink dress from the Michael Kors spring line that fit her voluptuous curves to perfection. Matching pink stilettos adorned her feet. Kenzie was always elegant and stylish while Nina tended to go for more flamboyant clothes like the Alexander McQueen black-and-yellow print dress she currently wore. Shoes were her downfall. She loved unusual shoes and the pair she wore with her dress today were shaped like fish with the mouth as the toe and the heels looking like fins.

"When are you coming to work for me and make my new casino and hotel the hippest place on the planet?" Miss E. asked.

Nina chuckled. "I have never planned a media campaign for a casino before."

Kenzie nudged her good-naturedly. "You'd do a terrific job. You always do. Look at how you saved Sam Beaumont's career. That man was dead-drunk, facedown in his own vomit on Sunset Boulevard. And now he's an Oscar winner. Why? Because you knew how to clean up his reputation and make him bankable again. You Nina'd him."

Nina clapped her hands. "I'm a verb."

"And Restaurant des Roux used to be a burger joint," Kenzie continued. "And now a line wraps around the block with people who want to get in and eat thirty-dollar hamburgers. That was one brilliant media campaign."

"I need your magic touch." Miss E. glanced around the restaurant and waved at Nina's mother who waved back and started to weave her way to the table.

Nina opened her mouth, not certain what to say. A hotel/casino!

"And don't forget the new spa," Kenzie added. She leaned toward Nina. "My soon-to-be sister-in-law and my brother are converting the hot springs on the back of the property into a spa. They broke ground six weeks ago and the walls are already up. It's supposed to be completed by Christmas, barring any emergencies."

Nina had heard Hunter was engaged to be married. He and Donovan were the only Russell brothers she'd ever met. Scott never seemed to be around when she and Kenzie visited with Miss E. and now that their careers had gone in different directions, they barely got together more than once in a blue moon.

"I don't think I've ever seen Nina speechless before." Wry humor colored Kenzie's voice.

"What exactly do you want?" The fact that they'd come all the way from Reno meant this new project was really important. Nina had managed to do a little research about Reno and the Casa de Mariposa, which had given her a few ideas, but she needed more information.

A waitress came over to take Kenzie and Miss E.'s drink order. Nina saw that her mother had gotten distracted and stopped to talk to a friend.

"I want the Nina mojo." Miss E. laughed. "You made this place," she spread her arms wide to indicate Lua el Sol, "the place to be seen in LA. I want Casa de Mariposa the place to be seen in Reno." She waved her hand. "I've been here five minutes and already I've spotted an Oscar-winning director, an Emmy-award-winning actress and two musicians. In the corner over there is that Grammy-winning jazz band, which, by the way, I adore. And if I'm not mistaken, isn't that," she pointed at a center table, "one of the Monaco royals?"

Nina followed Miss E.'s gestures. She was so used to seeing the rich and famous that it never impacted on her. Lua el Sol was a fun place to come and be seen without being bothered. The paparazzi weren't allowed within three blocks so celebrities wouldn't have to shove their way through throngs of people to get in. They could have their meal in peace and enjoy the atmosphere.

"Miss E." Grace Torres finally arrived at the table clutching a platter of appetizers. She set the platter down in the center of the table just as the waitress brought the drinks.

"What have we here, Mama Torres?" Kenzie asked eyeing the food. Kenzie loved trying new foods and once told Nina every morsel that came out of her father's kitchen was amazing.

"Papa's experimenting in the kitchen again. The balls that look like crusty hush puppies are *acarajé*, shrimp with black-eyed peas and onions. These are *bolinhos de arroz* made with rice and fried. These little drumsticks are chicken *coxinha*." Grace's voice still held the cadence of her Alabama childhood. Tonight she had tucked a spray of yellow orchids in her hair to match her bright yellow dress.

"They look delicious," Kenzie said, her fork out ready to spear the shrimp.

"Our special tonight," Grace continued, "is a lovely black-bean stew called *feijoada* with *pão de queijo*, which is cheese bread. And for dessert we have *brigadeiros*, which are little chocolate-and-caramel truffles."

"Chocolaty caramel goodness," Kenzie gasped in delight. Kenzie had never met a chocolate-anything that she didn't devour. And Nina couldn't believe she was still a model-slim, perfect size four.

Grace patted Kenzie on the cheek. "I knew you were coming."

"I love you." Kenzie took a bite of the savory shrimp balls and moaned. "Incredible."

"You do realize you have to share, don't you?" Nina teased.

"You always were a spoilsport." When Kenzie pouted men turned to look.

"Enjoy," Grace said. "I will return with the next course in a little bit."

"Is your mother going to sing tonight?" Kenzie asked. "I'd hate to come all this way and miss your parents' music."

"She sings almost every night. And the great thing is you never know who's going to join in."

Miss E. clapped her hands. "That is what I want for the resort, Nina. This incredible joy and fun wrapped up in old-world elegance. Casa de Mariposa is a lovely lady, but dull and uninteresting. I want you to make her interesting."

"First, let's eat, dance, and if so inclined we'll sing.

And tomorrow I'll work out some ideas and come up on Wednesday to go over everything with you."

Miss E. filled her plate with an assortment of food and dug in. Nina had one hand on the plate and the other with her fork when a voice sounded behind her.

"Nina. Darling."

She turned to find her ex-husband Carl Durant standing behind her. Carl was a handsome man with whitish-blond surfer hair, dark blue eyes and a fine, blond stubble on his chin. He was impeccably dressed in black jeans and T-shirt. He'd told her once that wearing black made him look mysterious. Nina thought he looked ridiculous. The black made him look washed-out and tired.

Hanging on his arm was his newest love, the tiny, barely legal, bubblegum-blonde Tiffani Diamond he'd dumped Nina for. Tiffani wore a tight white dress with black shoes and clutch purse. The white did nothing for her fair complexion though she'd tried to make up for it with heavy eye makeup and her hair pulled into long ringlets about her face.

Nina pasted a half smile on her face, prepared to be nice to Carl.

"Carl, how…how's tricks?" Since their divorce, his career had nose-dived. He'd decided he didn't need her anymore since his career was made. How ironic. She tried not to gloat—it was bad karma. Maybe for a moment.

"I have a lot of balls in the air, juggling a lot of things. Just thought I'd drop by to say hello. And Tiffani here landed a part in *CSI*."

Nina leaned forward. "As a dead body?"

Tiffani stiffened with a glare at Nina

"Be nice, Nina," Carl chided softly.

"I thought I was. What brings you here?"

"Tiffani wanted some of your mother's quickies."

For a second, Nina had no idea what he meant. "You mean *quindim*." She was surprised Tiffani ate. She didn't look like she'd had a decent meal in years.

"Those coconut flans," Carl explained. "Tiffani loves them."

"Really, Tiffani," Kenzie said. "You eat?"

"Not since 2010." Nina was being nasty and knew it, but couldn't seem to play fair.

Tiffani flashed an angry scowl at Kenzie and Nina. "Come on, Carl. Maybe we should just leave."

"We just got here. This is the place to be, sweetie. Look, there's Benny Simmons. I hear he's looking for a new leading lady for his next show. Let's talk to him." Carl guided Tiffani away and Nina watched them glide toward Benny, who looked like he wanted to dive under the table.

"What did you see in him, Nina?" Miss E. asked curiously.

"Looking back, I loved his passion, his artistic vision and a part of me wanted to bring that to the world."

"So you were more in love with the possibilities rather than the realities." Kenzie studied Nina, a glimmer of sympathy in her eyes.

"I wanted us to create art together. But eventually money got in the way. And don't get me wrong. I understand about business and the adage 'you're only as good as your last film.' Carl started believing in the hype I worked into his media campaigns. He wanted the perfect Hollywood life and that included an up-and-coming actress, not me."

"Rule number one," Miss E. said sagely. "Never believe your own press."

"He stopped being grateful and started being demanding. He thought I would continue working on his career after he cheated on me and left me." Her parents had brought their vision of music to Hollywood and never compromised on it. "I saw him compromise his vision and our marriage. I felt hurt. Betrayed. He left me when I told him how disappointed I was in him. In his mind, I didn't have the right to be disappointed. While he was escorting Miss Tiffani around, I was supposed to get back on the train and keep promoting his career."

"You didn't, did you?" Miss E. asked.

"Not a chance. Since I quit being his marketing bitch, the only films he's gotten recently are *Space Dogs from Mars* and *Baby-Momma Slashers* and *Shark-A-Conda*."

"Would it be bad form if I snorted?" Miss E. said.

"Go ahead, you're not drinking," Nina said.

Miss E. snorted and Nina burst into laughter. "How poetic that the only offers he's getting are these films when he thought he was the next Scorsese. Who by the way, still takes my phone calls."

"That's a litter box moment," Miss E. said.

"I don't understand." Nina frowned.

"You were being catty, dear," Kenzie said with a pat on Nina's hand.

Nina found her gaze straying to Carl and Tiffani. Her mother had gently pried them away from Benny Simmons and eased them to an empty table nearest the dance floor. Benny looked relieved and Tiffani looked disappointed.

"You know he's not going to stop hounding you." Miss E.'s gaze had followed Nina's and she studied Carl and Tiffani.

"I had that impression."

"You should come to Reno and put yourself out of his sphere."

"So my taking the job and coming to Reno would be doing me a favor for my mental well-being." Nina grinned at Miss E.

"Exactly. He'd be too stupid to find you in Reno."

"He's not stupid. His problem is that his ego wins over his intelligence every time."

"Don't worry, dear, you'll find love again," Miss E. said with a sympathetic pat on Nina's hand.

"I know," Nina said with a sigh. "I like to think of him as my training-wheels husband."

"At least you found a husband, unlike some people I can name." Miss E. directed a gaze at Kenzie.

"Granny, don't even start," Kenzie said, warning in her tone, one finger held up.

"I was referring to your brothers, Scott and Donovan."

"Miss E., Hunter is getting married. That's the best we can do at the moment." Kenzie shook her head with a sigh, though her lips quivered with laughter.

"You guys are just a funny as ever." Nina grinned widely at Kenzie and Miss E. She'd always felt comfortable around Miss E. and Kenzie, despite the tragedy in their lives. Kenzie and her brothers had Miss E. to fall back on. Nina's family wasn't so different. Her parents shared the same values with Miss E. "I need to juggle some things around. I can be in Reno on Wednesday. That gives me enough time to flesh some ideas." She could do this.

"I know you'll come up with a powerful campaign." Miss E. rubbed her hands together. "I can barely wait."

"I hope you'll be pleased." Nina's fingers itched for her iPad, but she'd left it in the car. "What about your brothers? I know Hunter has already taken charge of the new spa. What about Donovan and Scott? I've never met Scott in all the years we've known each other."

Kenzie leaned her elbows on the table. "Donovan is taking over the restaurants and updating the menus. Scott is done playing army man and is taking over security.

He's back in DC right now, packing up his condo and getting it ready to be sold. He should be back in another week or so."

"And what about your job at Saks?" Nina queried Kenzie.

Kenzie grinned. "I'm working for the family now."

"I can't believe you're leaving Manhattan."

"Already done. Sold my apartment two weeks ago and I already have a lot of ideas for updating the boutiques."

Mama Torres returned to the table, a plate in her hands.

"We're spiriting your daughter away to Reno, Grace," Miss E. said.

"Good, she needs to get out of this town for a while." She set the plate on the table. "And now for dessert."

"Chocolate," Kenzie said reverently.

"Share," Nina warned.

Kenzie frowned. "If you insist."

Mama Torres distributed the tiny chocolate *brigadeiros*. Kenzie looked like she'd just died and gone to heaven. Her eyes practically rolled back in her head as she took a delicate bite of one of the candies. "Oh. Oh. This is... Words just aren't enough."

"Heavenly," Nina finished for her.

Scott Russell stood in the center of his empty living room, looking around to make sure he hadn't forgotten anything. He owned very little. Military life did that to a person. Scott had never been someone to accumulate possessions. Everything he had was currently packed in a half dozen boxes, sitting in a stack by the front door ready to be loaded into his car. He wasn't coming back.

The apartment was small, but he liked it. The living room opened to a balcony overlooking a tiny courtyard he'd shared with the family in the apartment below.

Danny Esposito opened a closet and looked inside.

Danny was a tall, lean man with wavy black hair, deceptively calm brown eyes and olive skin showing his Latin parentage. They had met in Iraq and been friends ever since. When Danny jumped from military security to private security by starting his own firm, Scott had gone with him.

"Looks like you have everything," Danny said closing the closet door.

"Not much to show for three years in one place." Scott wondered how his footprint could be so small in such a large world.

"I'm the same way," Danny replied. "You ready?"

"Yeah." Scott opened the door and Danny maneuvered the dolly, piled with the boxes, through the door.

"I'm going to miss you, Scott," Danny said.

"Yeah, me, too." They reached his SUV parked in the carport to the side of the apartment building. Scott unlocked it and opened the rear hatch. The two of them shoved boxes in. After he closed the rear hatch, he and Danny leaned against it for a moment.

The day was warm, but overcast. Scott heard the distant rumble of thunder and knew the predicted storm was on its way. A few tentative drops splashed the asphalt.

"Reno is the ends of the earth, man," Danny said.

"No," Scott replied. "The Hindu Kush is the ends of the earth."

Danny chuckled. Silence fell between them. Scott listened to the sounds of traffic on the roadway outside along with the distant roll of thunder.

Washington, DC, was a city that didn't sleep. In a way, Scott would miss the energy, the sense of history being made and the undercurrent of power pervading the city. He wouldn't miss the traffic, the crowds or the politicians who too often made his life miserable.

"Why Reno?"

"Because you've never met my grandmother." Scott pushed his hands into the pockets of his jeans. "When she wants something, it happens." And right now she needed him. After spending the last few weeks at the casino, studying it, looking for ways to improve security, Scott could almost understand why his grandmother wanted it. "Reno and Miss E. have a lot in common. Reno has this sense of being wild and untamed. My grandmother is sort of the same."

"I don't know, Scott." Danny shook his head.

"Come for a visit and take a look at the city. You'll see. Reno is just different. And I like it. I didn't think I would, but I do." The pace was different and the people were different. Reno had no illusions about what kind of city it was. Washington, DC, was all about illusions.

A rumble of thunder sounded again. The rain increased in intensity until the sound of it on the metal roof of the carport sounded like gunshots.

Scott didn't regret quitting his job. He was tired of self-important senators who thought they could get away with anything. He was tired of the political games that made the government look like *Saturday Night Live*. At times he felt like he was dealing with five-year-olds in ten-thousand-dollar suits. And watching their bratty, over-privileged children was like riding herd on Chihuahuas.

Suddenly he was anxious to get on the road. The drive to Reno would take four days, driving ten hours a day. He planned to make it in three.

He and Danny shook hands. Scott watched Danny climb into his SUV and drive away. Scott stood in the alley looking up at his apartment. He'd made his decision to leave. He'd lived a gypsy lifestyle long enough. The time had come to settle into something more stable. He'd felt for a while that something was missing in his life, he just wasn't sure what.

A Cadillac Escalade roared down the alley and slammed to a stop in front of him. Water sprayed his shoes and he glanced down in irritation. The driver's door opened and Anastasia Parrish jumped out.

"My father told me you quit your job and you're leaving Washington."

Scott's eyes narrowed. Twenty-five-year-old Anastasia Parrish, daughter of Senator Richard Parrish, was tall with pixie-cut brown hair, brown eyes with a touch of green and skin the color of braised almonds. She was also crazy. Scott had been hired to keep her out of trouble while her father ran for re-election. Keeping her out of trouble had turned into a job and a half.

"How do you know where I live?"

She shrugged elegant shoulders. "I looked you up on Google."

"Then Google your way home."

"How can you leave me? I'm in the middle of a crisis." Drama poured off her in waves.

"Of your own making," Scott said.

"But Scott, I need you." She touched his arm.

Scott stepped away. "Get back in your car and go home, Miss Parrish." Pretty as a picture and crazy as a loon, that was Anastasia Parrish in a nutshell.

"Let me come with you." She looked dejected. "You're the only one who understands me. You saved me from that stalker."

"And your stalker is in jail, you're safe, and my job is done."

"What do I do if he escapes?" She turned desperate eyes on him.

"Tell your dad and he'll hire protection. The company I used to work for will be happy to help you again."

"But I want you."

"I don't work for them any longer."

Tears gathered in her eyes and dripped down her cheeks. "You can work for me privately."

A lot of the guys he'd worked with would have been happy to be Princess Anastasia's sex toy. Scott wasn't one of them. Behind that gorgeous face, beautiful body and designer wardrobe was a lost little girl with major daddy issues and his job wasn't to find her.

"But, Scott," she pleaded.

"Go home, Miss Parrish, call your therapist and talk to him." He opened the car door.

"Please, don't go. Daddy needs you. I need you. I think I love you."

What she needed was a good psychiatrist. Though he was probably better than the rock singer, the polo champion, the reality star or the football player she was frequently seen with—at least he wouldn't take advantage of her.

He took her by the arm and led her back to her car, rain pouring down on them. "Go home, Miss Parrish." He opened the car door and pushed her inside. He closed the door and walked back to his car.

She stared at him for a moment, then started the car, put it in gear and drove off.

He stood in the rain watching her drive away. Water dripped down the back of his jacket, plastering his shirt to his skin. He felt sorry for Anastasia Parrish. She had everything money could buy, but she didn't have what she needed, a father who cared about her and a mother who didn't brush her off and tell her to make an appointment.

He got in his SUV, started the engine and backed out of the carport. Time to get on the road. Miss E. was waiting.

Chapter 2

Nina had never been to Reno. The closest she'd been was Lake Tahoe, where her parents used to rent a cabin during the summer months for a family getaway. From the moment the cab deposited her in front of the hotel, she knew she was going to love Reno.

The challenge of bringing a casino back to life excited her. She loved the thrill of new jobs. Though her previous jobs had been in the arena of up-and-coming actors or new movie releases, the idea of taking on a casino was another door opening in her career. Another opportunity that put her a step further away from her ex-husband who'd weighed in on not taking this job. Nina had ignored him. He had no say in her future, not anymore, not after he dumped her for Tiffani.

As a media expert, Nina traveled the world, though her base of operations was Hollywood. Hollywood was home and she loved the energy and excitement the city had. In Hollywood or any other place she'd worked in before, she could just pick up a phone and invite a dozen people to lunch. But in Reno, she knew no one except her best friend, Kenzie Russell.

At her feet her dog whimpered. The tiny affenpinscher had been a gift from Carl and she loved the little dog. King

Kong pressed his tiny black nose against the mesh of his carrier. She reached down to gently stroke it.

"We're here." She kept her tone soothing and calm as she walked into the cool hotel, happy to be out of the heat while the bellhop trailed behind her hauling a trolley piled high with her luggage.

"Nina," Kenzie called, waving.

"It is hot here." Nina placed Kong's carrier on the floor next to her feet.

"But you're going to love it." Kenzie laughed and reached over to hug Nina. "Welcome to Reno, Nevada, the biggest little city in the west. You look fabulous. That is an original Alexander McQueen."

Nina smoothed a hand down the black-and-white houndstooth pattern of her silk dress. "You look pretty fab yourself."

Kenzie wore a mint-green sheath with matching shoes that perfectly accented her dark brown eyes and mocha skin. Her long brown hair was swept up into a casual ponytail.

"What do you think?" Kenzie asked, spreading her arms wide.

"I'm still taking everything in." Nina's first impression of the Casa de Mariposa Hotel was one of sedate beauty of an old-world kind. It had good bones, but it needed something more. Something dramatic.

As she walked through the reception area into the casino she studied the clientele. She was struck by the lack of people under the age of thirty. Most of the stools in front of the slot machines were occupied by older men and women.

Nina tried to keep her mind open, but a stroll out to the pool showed only a couple families with young children, a few teenagers splashing in the deep end of the pool and older couples sunning themselves on the decks.

She strolled back inside, her thoughts churning, only half listening to Kenzie's chatter.

After checking in and arranging for her luggage to be delivered to her suite, she allowed Kenzie to take her out to the pool. Nina parked herself on a stool at the bar. Kong whined from the depths of her tote bag. Nina absently patted him as she sipped the iced tea the bartender brought her. He also brought a small bowl of water for Kong.

"I know you haven't unpacked yet, but…what do you see?" Kenzie parked herself on the stool next to Nina.

Nina took her time answering. "I see a lot of people in their forties, fifties and older, but not many younger. If you want to make this hotel casino attractive to young, hip people you need to offer the activities they want."

"Which would be…?"

"You're young and hip, what do you want?"

"To eat ice cream and not worry about my thighs." Kenzie glanced down at her legs.

"I've seen your thighs," Nina said with a laugh. "You don't need to worry about them."

"As a young woman racing toward thirty, I want to go to a nightclub. I want to have fun." Kenzie frowned as she considered Nina's question. "I want trendy shopping, high-energy shows with A-list celebrities, along with luxury, great food, glitz, glamour and cool." Kenzie paused. "Everybody wants to be cool."

"In other words, Miss E. wants to keep the elegance while attracting a younger crowd without losing her over-forty regulars. She wants to be the epicenter of Reno."

"It needs glamour." Kenzie pointed at Nina. "It needs you."

"Stop." Nina held up her hand. "You don't need to flatter me. I'm all in. You're my best friend and I adore your grandmother. She knows there's a winner beneath the stodgy façade of this casino. I have a ton of ideas."

"I know you are creative, but Miss E. did tell you that New Year's Eve is the deadline. She wants to have the grand reopening then."

"I have her notes. Once we decide on a theme, I'll have a whole campaign worked out and ready to implement in a couple days."

"The theme is the problem. Miss E. is having a difficult time thinking about a theme that will attract the guests she wants to attract."

"I have several concepts in mind that I think will fit her idea of elegant and classy along with fun, glamorous and sexy." She dug her tablet out of the tote. A half-unwrapped ball of yarn, a knitting needle trapped inside it, came with it.

"What are you knitting?" Kenzie asked curiously.

"Still knitting booties for my friends' babies." Nina had started knitting as a way to keep her fingers busy while she thought, and found it relaxing.

She rerolled the ball of yarn and tucked it back in her tote bag. She tapped her tablet where she'd already put together a couple slide shows. Nina had put together other campaigns in a shorter time with less to work with. She'd never done a casino before, but the structure of a campaign was generally the same. She came up with the ideas and found people to help her implement them.

Nina turned her tablet computer to Kenzie so she could see some of her ideas. "Let's take a look. Las Vegas offers luxury, glamour and cool at a number of different levels. Caesar's Palace, Bellagio, Luxor and the MGM Grand offer luxury, high-end dining, entertainment and shopping. Circus Circus, Treasure Island and Excalibur offer family fun and activities. Hard Rock offers trendy with great headliners in the rock-and-roll arena. But what they all provide is different ways to play. People go to Las Vegas to eat too much, drink too much, shop too much, and basically they went everything at a *too much* level." Nina tapped the tablet. "Reno doesn't draw the same international crowd. It's more difficult to get to. It has less variety than Vegas. But these are things that can work in your favor. If you give people what they need here, they won't go elsewhere to experience it."

"What will we offer?"

Nina thought for a moment. "Exclusivity. What Robert Redford did for Park City with the Sundance Festival, I'm going to do for Miss E., but with all-year-long activities."

"You are ambitious, girl," Kenzie said, her eyes wide with amazement.

"'Ambition bites the nails of success,' according to Bono." Nina grinned. The bartender brought her another iced tea and a platter of fruit. She picked at the fruit. "You know, if we weren't working, we'd be drinking mimosas."

Kenzie joined Nina in laughter.

Nina's gaze was caught by a man skirting the pool area. He wore khaki cargo pants, a white polo shirt and military boots. "Wow." He was hot.

"Hey, that's Scott." Kenzie waved vigorously, catching his attention.

When she'd first met Kenzie, he'd been out saving the world and somehow in between they'd never been on the same schedule.

She waved again, and the man veered toward them.

Kenzie jumped off her stool and ran to him, enveloping him in a huge hug. "You're back." She dragged him to the bar.

Nina couldn't stop staring. She was used to being around pretty, good-looking guys, but this one looked fabulous without all the effort.

"This is Nina," Kenzie said. "Nina, this is Scott."

"The famous Nina Torres." Scott's voice was deep and authoritative.

"That would be me." Her heart skipped a beat as she slipped off the stool and gazed up at him. He was tall and broad shouldered. Nina, at five-seven, felt dwarfed by him.

"Nice to finally meet you." He held out a hand and shook hers. "When you have a few moments, we need to talk."

An electrical jolt radiated through her fingers at his touch. Breathless, she gazed at him unable to look away. He was, by far, the best looking of the Russell brothers, with his sharp-featured face, eyes the color of Baltic amber and close-cropped black hair. The fact that he obviously worked out was not lost on her as she tried not to stare at his muscles.

Kong suddenly barked. Nina turned around to soothe him.

Scott's eyes narrowed. He stared at the dog. "What the hell kind of dog is that? It looks like a monkey."

"That's Kong. He's an affenpinscher. It means monkey terrier."

Scott gave the dog a strange look.

"Are you judging me by my dog?" Nina asked.

"No," he replied.

"Liar."

"I have this thing about little dogs."

"He has the heart of a lion." Nina picked him up out of her tote and petted him gently. Kong snuggled against her chest. "And he's very loyal."

Carl had chosen the breed because he felt its personality was similar to hers. His explanation had amused her. That was the man she'd fallen in love with. He'd been sincere, determined and romantic, traits that evaporated later in their marriage. She'd mourned the loss of that man. Fame had killed him and she had been partially responsible for the megalomaniac he'd turned into. His new fame revealed his demons.

"Have you come up with any plans for your media blitz?" Scott asked.

Nina grinned at his abrupt change in subject. "I have a few." She wasn't quite ready to reveal them. "I want to talk to Miss E. first."

"Nothing that's going to cause security nightmares, right?"

"Where's your sense of adventure?" Nina teased. Kenzie turned away to hide her own grin. She'd always said Scott was the serious one and everyone delighted in tweaking him a little bit.

"I left it in Afghanistan."

"Let's schedule a meeting after I've talked to Miss E. Right now I want to look over the hotel and the casino and experience it in all its stages."

"Experience away," he said. "And don't miss the magic show."

Kenzie sighed. "I definitely have that on the agenda."

Nina glanced at her friend. "That doesn't sound too enthusiastic."

"You haven't met Marvin the Marvelous." Scott laughed. He kissed his sister on the cheek. "I'll catch you later. I'm still unpacking." He sauntered off.

Nina found herself watching him cross the pool area and enter the hotel. He looked nice, but he was going to be trouble.

"That was interesting." Kenzie stared after her brother, her brow furrowed in thought.

"What do you mean?"

"I think my big brother just pulled your metaphoric pigtails."

Nina's eyebrows rose. "I beg your pardon."

"I think he likes you."

"He thinks my dog is stupid," Nina scoffed, petting Kong soothingly. Kong licked her chin.

"He only says stupid things when he likes a girl."

"So insulting my dog means he likes me. Is he still in kindergarten?"

"Don't get me wrong." Kenzie shook her head. "He does very well with the ladies—he just doesn't have them in his life long-term."

"Number one, I would never date my best friend's brother. And number two, I don't have time." She deposited Kong back in her purse. "Shall we go on with our tour? I have a hankering to see Marvin the Marvelous."

After the tour, Nina sat in a corner booth in the bar and made notes on her tablet. Every idea she had she jotted down. She sipped a dirty martini and nibbled on a bowl of pretzels. A bartender wiped down the bar. A cocktail waitress in a short black flamenco-type skirt and white blouse worked her way around the few filled tables.

The bar was sad in a way. It was all dark woods, Spanish arches and too much space, the kind of bar a person went to when they didn't want to be bothered. If she were in charge of making it over, she'd decrease the size and make it more intimate. She'd reduce the lighting and put cute little lamps on the tables so that only the people sitting down would be highlighted. She'd make it romantic. Romance could sell anything.

Chimes from the casino filtered into the bar. She watched a couple at another table. The woman was dressed to kill for two in the afternoon in a low-cut dress, hair pulled to the side over her shoulder and a lipstick that was just too red. The man watched her with avid interest. Nina couldn't figure out what was wrong with the two of them.

Scott appeared in the entryway and for a second, Nina's heart raced. Just looking at him made her tingle all over in a way she'd never felt before.

Scott saw her and gave her a smile. "Can I join you?"

Nina nodded even as her gaze wandered back to the woman at the other table.

He slid into the booth across to her and saw the look on her face. "She's a hooker. If that's what you're wondering."

"How can you tell?"

"She's wearing stockings and a garter belt. And her body language is very seductive, but practiced. She's not into him, she's into his wallet." Scott signaled a waitress and ordered coffee. "Every woman under twenty-five in this room is a working girl, except for the waitresses."

"And how do you know this?" Prostitution was rampant in Los Angeles, but working women were not allowed in her parents' restaurant. Her father had a sixth sense the moment he saw a woman and knew if she was working or not. Politely, he would ask her to leave.

"The bartenders get a percentage of their fees."

"But prostitution is legal in Nevada."

"Only on a county-by-county basis. It's illegal here in Washoe County. Reno is a no-ho zone." Scott smiled at the waitress when she set the coffee down in front of him.

Nina tried not to laugh, but a small chuckle escaped anyway. Scott was a military man and his directness was refreshing. "What are you going to do about it?"

"For the moment, I'm taking notes, scouting the bartending schools and talking to the Reno PD. See that waitress over there? She's an undercover vice cop."

"I get where you're coming from and you want to clean this place up…"

"Before the grand opening," he interjected.

"And I get it's against the law, but aren't women like her why men come to places like this?"

"That is a very good question."

"Do you have a very good answer for me?" She tilted her head at him.

"Controlled hedonism."

"What do you mean by that?"

"There has to be a line. And this is the line. Those women and what they do is on the wrong side of the line. I'm not judging what they're doing, but what they do isn't going to be allowed to happen here because it reflects badly on this hotel and therefore reflects badly on my grandmother."

"You sound just like my dad." She could hear her father's voice clearly in her head making the same statement about how people let their standards slip and there went the neighborhood.

"Is your dad a cop? I thought he owned a nightclub."

"He owns a nightclub, but sometimes I think it's his own personal police state. And he rules his restaurant with an iron martini shaker. By the way, this is the best martini I've ever had. Can't you just give the guy a slap on the wrist and let him off with a warning?"

"Why are you drinking a martini at two in the afternoon?"

"I'm checking his skills. This is work-related alcohol consumption. I need to find a spin on ways to promote this place. The best martini this side of the Rockies is great advertising."

"You think a martini would bring business."

Nina sighed. "Two years ago, I was hired to promote

this little microbrewery in New York and last month it was bought out by a major food corporation. The former owner just bought a piece of Saint Lucia and is lying on the beach soaking up the sun."

"Basically, you're a rainmaker."

Nina shrugged. "I don't really have a title. I'm just good at promotions. I create buzz and have a knack for understanding how media works." Knowing what people wanted was what she had always been good at.

"How do you make a living out of that?" Scott looked interested.

"By knowing the people who are right for what you need. Right now my friend Eydie is working up a website for the hotel. She's a master at websites and blogs. We've already outlined a dozen blogs talking about different aspects of the hotel and the amenities. And more blogs about the Reno area in general. I'm thinking about contests, because people like to win things. This is basic stuff. I'm going to call friends of mine and talk them into coming here to party for New Year's. And they'll come if Miss E. throws in a free room, a limo from the airport and some gambling money." Which they would all lose in the first hour. Nina didn't gamble unless it was the penny or nickel slots. The few times she'd been to Las Vegas, every coin she fed into the machine was a penny that didn't work for her.

"Friends, as in who?"

"Celebrities to be named later."

"That's a whole lot of free."

"Not everything will be for free and they will pay for it especially when they see what they get out of it."

"And what's that?"

"Exposure." Every celebrity Nina knew would do anything for exposure. Exposure reminded them of who they were and what they'd accomplished even if they were no longer the darlings of Hollywood.

"Let's talk about the security nightmares of having these people here?" Scott tapped the table with his index finger.

"A lot of them will bring their own security and staff. And before you start worrying, let me do what I need to do and then I'll talk to you about security."

Scott simply frowned, shaking his head.

"I can see you're worried," Nina said, "but can we come back to this later when I have more information?"

Scott nodded, finished his coffee and slid out of the booth. "Then I'll let you get back to work."

Nina watched him leave, appreciating the tight, muscular body and the way he stalked with the confidence of an alpha wolf. Then her thoughts turned back to the hotel. As much as she loved watching Scott, she was here to do a job.

Scott returned to his office. The idea of celebrities running around the hotel didn't please him. He didn't like working with them. In Washington, the people he protected expected to be targets, acted accordingly and trusted him to keep them safe. Celebrities knew they could be targets, but the nature of their careers was to be seen and they dealt with a lot of yes people who never disagreed with them or considered their safety as long as their faces showed up on the next internet feed. God save him. For all Nina's assertions that things would be fine, she didn't understand that not only would he be dealing with the rich and famous and their bad behavior but their security teams and their staff.

He rubbed his temples, a headache threatening. What the devil was Miss E. thinking bringing Hurricane Nina on board? While the casino wasn't bringing in a lot of profit, it wasn't losing money. Did Miss E. really need this extra spin?

His job was going to be huge regardless of who was here, because somewhere underneath the surface of the casino, something wasn't quite right. But he couldn't put his fingers on it, just that his gut told him something dysfunctional was going on. And having Nina around distracted him. She was sexy, exotic and bold with a level of energy that didn't seem to have a cap. He wanted to put everything down and follow her. She was sandy beaches, tall, icy drinks and sex in a hammock. Not that he'd ever had sex in a hammock, but Nina made him think about it.

He opened the door that led from his office to the control room. The room was large to accommodate rows of monitors with men sitting in front of them keeping an eye on the activity in the casino, the bars and the restaurants.

"Anything going on that I should know about?" Scott asked Gary White who oversaw the control room.

"The usual," Gary White said. "Everything's good." He was average height with pale skin and reddish-brown hair. He never looked directly at Scott. His gaze continually slipped to the left or the right, making Scott wonder what he was hiding.

Scott knew nothing was good. Gary White was on his list of dysfunctional security people who had to go. He was sloppy and lazy. Security guards needed to be licensed. From what Scott had been able to deduce, his license had expired. Scott needed to be careful on how he got rid of people. The unions were powerful and he didn't want them as an enemy. Right now, he'd be gathering evidence and documenting Gary's offenses. He had to walk a tightrope and unlike Hurricane Nina, who wanted things done yesterday, he had to record everything to show cause.

"Will you take a look at that?" Gary pointed at one of his monitors.

Scott leaned over and felt his stomach turn into knots. "What the hell is she doing here?"

"You know her, boss?"

"My worst nightmare." Scott volunteered no more information. His headache went from mild to threat-level red.

Anastasia Parrish stood in the lobby surrounded by a half dozen Louis Vuitton suitcases. She held her Chihuahua in her arms as she stood at the desk with an imperious look on her petulant face, waiting for the reception clerk to check her into her room. She wore a white pantsuit that looked as though it had just come off the Paris runway, with oversize sunglasses.

She took the glasses off and fluffed her dark brown hair with one hand.

His first thought was to run down to the lobby and confront her, nipping this crap in the bud. But after a moment's thought, he decided ignoring her was better. If anything, Anastasia hated being ignored. Daddy's little girl thought the world turned on her nickel and was happy enough to tell anyone who would listen.

"Nice friend, boss," Gary White said with a knowing chuckle.

Scott glared at the man and didn't answer.

The door opened and his brother, Hunter, poked his head in. "Got a second, bro?"

Scott nodded and stepped out of the control room. Before his brother could say something, Scott's cell phone rang. The front desk was calling him.

"Scott Russell here," he said knowing what the receptionist's next comment would be.

"Mr. Russell, a Miss Anastasia Parrish is asking for you," came a chirpy voice.

"I'm a little bit busy right now." Scott pinched the bridge

of his nose. "Tell Miss Parrish I will have to speak with her later."

"Very well, sir." The woman disconnected.

Scott shoved his phone back in his pocket. His brother watched him curiously.

"Miss Parrish. Anastasia Parrish, spoiled rotten daughter of Senator Parrish?"

"Yeah," Scott replied. "The bane of my existence."

"She's very beautiful."

"She's spoiled, petty and mean." Scott leaned against the wall. How the hell was he going to get rid of her? "She's twenty-five but acts like she's thirteen, which is ridiculous. She thinks she's in love with me."

"She's pretty enough," Hunter said. "Though compared to Lydia, she's kind of colorless."

"Any woman you look at is colorless compared to Lydia." Scott's brother had finally found the love of his life in Lydia Montgomery. They were engaged to be married.

"What are you going to do?" Hunter asked.

"I don't have many options. This is my home and she's invaded it. I need to convince her to head back to Washington, DC, and just leave me alone." Scott felt annoyed and beyond irritated. As though he didn't have enough headaches, now he had to deal with Anastasia. She was poison.

"Before you hide in your office—" Hunter held up an envelope "—I'm going to need your security plans for the spa. The electricians are coming on Monday and I want to make sure we have enough security cameras in all the right places."

"Okay," Scott said, relieved to put Anastasia on the back burner for the moment. "Let's check out the blueprints again and I'll go over the areas I've already earmarked for security cameras."

Hunter started walking down the hall. Scott followed. He thought he heard a dog barking, but after a moment decided it was just his imagination.

Chapter 3

When Nina said she'd meet Miss E. in her office, the last thing she expected was an RV in the parking garage with cords attaching it to the side of the building. The RV was a lot more opulent than the vehicles Nina had seen at various RV shows. The blue-and-green interior consisted of a living area, a tiny galley and a large bedroom at the end. The door to the tiny bathroom was closed.

Miss E. sat on a greenish-blue sofa, lips pursed as she studied Nina's iPad on the hardwood coffee table. Next to her was Lydia Montgomery, Miss E.'s business partner.

Lydia Montgomery was a tiny, fragile-looking woman with a wealth of hair clustered about her shoulders, intelligent brown eyes and a classically beautiful face. She wore a white-and-black Stella McCartney pantsuit. She was stylish in a Lena Horne/Princess Diana way that made Nina want to make her the face of Casa de Mariposa.

"Is there any way I can turn you into a celebutante?" Nina asked her.

Lydia's elegant eyebrows rose in surprise. "What?"

"A celebutante. Sort of like Paris Hilton, but with class."

Lydia shook her head, amusement in her eyes. "No."

Nina sighed. It was worth a try. "Understand this is all tentative." She pointed at her tablet. "I want to create a buzz that establishes Casa de Mariposa as an insider place that you need to be totally cool to get into. And everyone will want to come because deep down inside, people want to be cool, to be unique. They want to be part of the 'in' crowd."

Lydia nodded, as though agreeing.

"Vegas has such a great tag line. 'What happens in Vegas stays in Vegas.' That is so alluring a concept. At the city limits you can let yourself be free. But now that Vegas is everyone's playground, there's no place to be naughty anymore. We need to bring that concept to Reno."

"Do you mean you want people to come to Reno to misbehave and do bad things?" Miss E. frowned as she studied the tablet.

"I want people to come here and be naughty." Being naughty was good, Nina thought.

Lydia frowned. "What's the difference?"

"Naughty is fun without the jail time." Nina grinned at Lydia.

"What's your plan of attack?" Miss E. asked as she studied the tablet.

"A good website and a great blogger. I have a friend, Eydie, who already has worked up a mock website and blog." Nina ran her fingers across the iPad and started the slide show. "I looked at other hotel websites and they all spotlight what's happening in their hotel or casino, but don't really give a flavor for Reno. Besides highlighting the hotel, spa and casino, we also show life in Reno away from the casinos. I know I've only been here a day, but this place has an incredible foundation. Once the spa is completed, you'll have some of the best amenities to offer guests and I know how to entice them to come." She had more ideas, but didn't want to give too much away too soon.

Miss E. nodded. "How are you going to get famous people to come here?"

Nina laughed. "They all owe me favors. I have several events the hotel should think about hosting."

"Such as?" Lydia asked.

"A film festival is one. This is an ideal location. You have a big jazz concert here every year and a film is a perfect complement to it. Who can resist movies and jazz? We could do a comic convention."

"Reed would like that," Miss E. said in delight.

"I know, I did my research. And I know from a friend that the snowboarding and ski people are looking for a new place to host their convention. The spillover would benefit every hotel in Reno."

"These are big plans," Lydia interrupted. "How are you going to implement them?"

Nina grinned. "With style and grace. I have an incredible group of people I work with and each one is a master at what they do. By the time we're done, Casa de Mariposa will be the place for every celebrity who wants to be seen, to be seen in."

Lydia frowned. "Aren't you concerned that Reno is a little difficult to get to? Anyone who wants to fly in has to change planes at least once, if not twice, depending on their start point."

"Not at all. Part of the appeal of Reno is the fact that it's slightly out of the way, giving it a sense of exclusivity. Anyone can take a direct flight to Vegas and be there in hours. Getting to Reno takes a little extra effort, but you, Miss E., are going to make that effort worthwhile."

"Look at you flattering me," Miss E. said with a wry shake of her head.

"The harder something is to attain, the more people want it. So it's a little more difficult to get here. Celebrities will come because they'll think it's a little more private.

And other people will come to see celebrities, so they'll make the effort, too."

"I get that we want to bring in celebrity guests," Lydia said, "because they'll bring the crowd, but we don't want to alienate any of our regular guests."

"I understand completely and I don't want to alienate them, either. The regular guests are the bread and butter of this place, yet at the same time, they want a show. And having celebrities stay here is a show you don't have to pay a lot for. You will have to compensate them in free rooms and free meals. These are people who play hard. You'll get them to your gaming tables, cocktail bars, restaurants and nightclub."

"How do you know this?" Lydia asked curiously.

"Lua el Sol has been the 'in' place for celebrities to be seen for over twenty years. I learned what I needed to know about making a place popular by watching my parents and instituting their strategies. I'm very good at what I do." And her parents were brilliant. Her father knew exactly how to make Lua el Sol the perfect hangout while providing great food, music and fun. She found her excitement growing. Before, she'd always had something to work with while promoting whoever or whatever she was promoting, but Casa de Mariposa had nothing. She had a clean slate to start with; she could build an incredible promotion from the ground up. Ideas swirled around her mind so quickly she could barely contain them.

"And you can get this in place for New Year's Eve, the grand opening."

"Done," Nina said proudly. "I thought for New Year's Eve we'd do a Brazilian-style *carnaval*, Rio in Reno. Samba dancing, Brazilian jazz and food. I thought I'd call my dad and have him sit down with Donovan…"

"Donovan," Miss E. said, "will be here in a few weeks.

He just has some things to take care of in Paris before he can get away."

"My dad will be happy to work with him on revamping the menu in the larger restaurant."

"I'm sure Donovan will be delighted." Miss E. looked delighted herself.

"Trust me," Nina patted Miss E.'s hand. "You have nothing to worry about."

"But isn't *carnaval* associated with Mardi Gras and Lent?" Lydia asked.

"We can start a new tradition." Nina wanted to shake things up a bit. Doing the same thing at the same time got old quickly. Nina's success was that she could take old events and make them new in an entirely different way. She liked the title "Rio in Reno." She envisioned a whole line of Rio-in-Reno events that would shake the foundations of the Casa de Mariposa.

Miss E. looked at Lydia. "I like it. I've always wanted to learn how to samba dance wearing one of those little, itty-bitty costumes with feathers."

Lydia sighed. "Four months ago, I would have been scandalized."

Nina grinned. "Miss E. has the body for it."

Lydia and Miss E. burst into laughter and Nina found herself joining in. Miss E. would do it. The first time Nina had met her, she'd known that Miss E. was a spitfire who held nothing back.

"What would the grandchildren say?" Lydia said between giggles.

Miss E. fell back against the sofa cushions. "They'd love it, except maybe for Scott. He's just too serious at times." She patted Nina's arm. "You need to loosen him up."

"Me! Why me?" Nina didn't think anything would loosen Scott's inner serious.

"Because you, my dear, are fun."

Nina's laughter trailed away, uncertain what to make of Miss E. comment. She and Scott were fire and rocks. All the two of them would do was make lava and level a city.

Scott stood behind Gary White, pointing at the monitor. "Did you see that?"

Gary leaned forward, frowning slightly. "She's Miles Dombrowsky's granny." Gary dismissed her with a wave of his hand. "She's here all the time and just as sweet as can be." Gary shrugged. "She's harmless. Brings cookies sometimes."

"Harmless?" Scott said. "She's stealing wallets." He eyed Gary, telling himself not to snarl at the man. Gary may have worked security in this casino for nearly ten years, but he didn't seem to know a thing about security. Or maybe he did, but was willing to let certain things slide because she was related to another employee.

"I'll call Miles and have him pick her up." Gary reached for his cell phone.

"I don't think so." Age was the greatest cover Scott had ever seen. Who would suspect a little old lady of being a thief who looked like she'd melt a heart of stone?

The elderly woman held a huge black tote and wore an oversize black hat with droopy pink flowers. She leaned over a man sitting at a slot machine, not quite touching him. Her hand moved so quickly Scott almost blinked. The little old lady was good with smooth, unhurried movements. If he hadn't been watching, expecting her next move, he might have missed it.

The elderly woman shuffled away. She moved out of the range of one security camera and into the next one. She stood in the center of the aisle between the rows of chiming slots, one hand to her chin, her eyes assessing the guests on stools in front of the machines.

Scott shook his head. Time to stop her. He spoke into the mic alerting the two security guards on the floor and told them to pick her up and bring her to the interview room. He watched as the two guards approached her and gently took her by the arm, ushering her discreetly from the floor.

Scott left the control room and headed for the interview room. A minute later, Michaelson and Turner brought her in.

"Take your hands off me, young man. How dare you manhandle me! I've been a loyal customer of this casino for over twenty-five years."

Scott simply smiled. "Please sit down." He pulled a chair out for her.

"You can't keep me here." She sat gingerly on the very edge of the chair, placing her tote on the table. "I've done nothing wrong." Her lower lips quivered. Tears gathered in the corners of her eyes and a tiny sob caught in her throat. "Why have you brought me here? I was minding my own business."

What a performance, Scott thought. He sat across from her smiling politely.

The woman was tiny, barely five feet tall, with delicate bone structure, a broad face, blue eyes and gray hair tucked tight inside the hat. A few wisps escaped and danced around her ears. She wore a plain gray dress belted at the waist, a gold watch on one wrist and a gold band on her left ring finger. Makeup, applied with expert skill, softened her face. He figured she was somewhere in her seventies, but a well-preserved seventies.

"I've got you on the monitor with your hand in a man's pocket."

"He was my grandson." She gave a shrug.

"No, he wasn't. Would you tell me your name?"

She lifted her chin into the air. "No comment."

He kept his voice soft and gentle. "Please, just tell me your name?"

"No." She stared stonily at him, her light blue eyes alive with amusement. She was enjoying herself. "You can't prove I've done anything wrong."

Scott rested his elbows on the table pretending to consider her comment. When he stood, he accidentally knocked her tote to the floor. Half a dozen wallets spilled out of the tote across the carpet.

The woman glanced down. "Those aren't mine."

"I know they aren't." He picked up the wallets and glanced inside each one.

"I don't know how those wallets got into my tote. They must have jumped in. Or someone else put them there. I'm being framed." She gave him a guileless look as though daring him to prove her wrong.

He opened a woman's wallet. Inside was a driver's license with her photo. Marina Dombrowsky. "Dombrowsky. Is that Polish?"

"Russian," she snapped, attempting to snatch the wallet out of his hand. He held it away from her.

"I see." He glanced at Turner. "I have a Miles Dombrowsky who works night security. That's an unusual enough name. Are you related to him?" He asked even though he already knew.

She pressed her lips together refusing to answer. Her eyes narrowed as she watched him. She knew he'd caught her red-handed, but she wasn't about to give an inch.

"Ms. Dombrowsky," he coaxed.

"Mrs. Dombrowsky," she snapped. "Married fifty-five years, God bless his miserly old soul, and gone these last three."

"Mrs. Dombrowsky," he corrected. "I'm going to do you a favor."

Her eyes narrowed. "What kind of favor?"

"I'm going to return all these wallets to their owners, no questions asked. You will be escorted from the building. Should I see your face here again, I'll be calling the Reno PD and turning you over to them."

She looked him straight in the eye with a defiant gleam. "Do your worst."

Scott smiled. "It's on, lady."

She sat straight in the chair, her gaze never leaving his face. He removed his cell phone and held it up. "Smile," he said and snapped a photo.

The flash blinded her and she blinked rapidly for a second. He sent the photo to his computer. He'd send it to everyone working security—the casino's own most-wanted list. "Now, I have your face for posterity. Trust me…" he pointed at her, feeling a little guilty for manhandling a little old lady "…I will not forget you ever."

She glared at him, her eyes slits and her mouth tight with anger. "You're a bully and you're rude."

"Ms. Dombrowsky…"

"Mrs. Dombrowsky," she snapped angrily.

"I don't want to find you in this casino ever again." He gathered up the wallets and turned to Turner as he left the room. "Take her home."

In his office he sat at his desk and called the reception desk asking them to page the names in the wallets. He'd take them down in a moment, but first he needed to make a note to have a talk with Miles Dombrowsky about his grandmother.

Nina walked into the restaurant. The room was huge, filled with booths lining the walls that were upholstered in browns and oranges. Large blocky tables with high-backed chairs sat in the center. The restaurant wanted to look Spanish, but didn't quite have the mood right. She already knew that Lydia Montgomery had some changes in mind to give the restaurant a more sophisticated ambience.

In a corner she saw Scott sitting by himself, his laptop open and a pile of papers surrounding it. She hesitated, wondering if he would be annoyed if she interrupted him, but decided he probably needed a break.

She walked up to him. "Mind if I join you?"

He looked up, his gaze unfocused. Then it sharpened into pleasure. "Sure. Have a seat."

"Don't overwhelm me with your enthusiasm." She slid into the booth across from him. The cushions were comfortable and she bounced a little settling herself in. She smiled at him, pleasure at the sight of him curling inside her. She wanted to smooth the furrow between his brows and say something to make him laugh.

"Then why did you ask?"

"Because this is the best table to people-watch."

A waitress approached with a menu. She wore a flouncy orange dress.

"That's why I sat here," Scott said.

"Who are you watching?" Nina perused the room critically. Most of the customers were older people with a few families interspersed. She glanced through the menu and found it uninspiring—mostly Mexican foods with standard American hamburgers and steaks. The menu needed a rehab.

"I'm watching everybody." His gaze darted around the room.

"Isn't that difficult? Don't you ever relax when you go out?" This man was in serious need of some fun.

"I can relax. There are times when I'm not working. This isn't one of them."

"What's going on in here that I'm not seeing? Is someone stealing the silverware?" She gazed around the room again. A man and woman sat with two children, coaxing them to eat. An elderly man flirted with his waitress while she served him food. A young couple who looked like they were honeymooners gazed into each other's eyes. In the opposite corner of the room in a shadowed booth, a man spoke on the phone and wrote something down in a notebook spread out on the table. Something about him seemed furtive.

"See that man in the opposite corner. He's taking bets on who's going to win the bachelor on *Project: Marriage*."

"The TV show!" Nina was a bit confused. "But gambling is legal."

"Sanctioned gambling, which means bets, need to be placed with licensed bookies in the casino and he's not licensed. The State of Nevada frowns on that and the casino frowns on it, too, since we're not making any money."

"What are you going to do?"

"A lot of people are going to get a free pass the first time."

"But what if they're doing something illegal? Shouldn't you call the police?" Nina frowned.

"You're the publicity expert. What do you think will happen?"

Nina thought for a moment. She'd had a lot of experience with people's arrest records and the unpleasant exposure that could bring. "An arrest is public record and can result in bad publicity."

"Exactly," Scott replied.

"Do these little problems occur in casinos? This morning you had the pickpocket…"

"You heard about that"

"Miss E. mentioned it."

"To some extent every casino has little problems, but a lot of what happens, or doesn't happen depends on the vigilance of the security force." He frowned.

Nina gazed around curiously. "This place seems to be having an epidemic."

He nodded, his eyes never leaving the unsanctioned bookie. The bookie shifted uncomfortably as though aware he was being watched.

"So what you're telling me," Nina continued, "is that security here is little bit lax."

"The security force here is a big part of the problem." He didn't elaborate.

The waitress returned. Nina ordered cheese-and-onion enchiladas and a glass of iced tea.

She watched the bookie. In between bites of food, he talked on the phone and wrote in his notebook. Nina noticed the waitress who took care of his table kept herself just out of reach when she checked on him. So the guy had wandering fingers, too.

"How are you going to fix things?" Nina asked curiously. She had a lot of events in the planning stages and each one would need to be safe.

"Eventually, I'll replace most of the security people here with my own choices."

"That's going to be tough. I got my talk about the unions earlier this afternoon."

"I support the unions. Don't get me wrong. But when a person is hired to do a job, they have to do it."

"I assume you're documenting everything."

"Exactly. Before I decided to check this out, I was in

the control room and saw four staff members place their own bets with Barney the bookie over there. Those guys will be easy to get rid of. They were on the clock using company time. And if I make a really big stink about it, it will prevent anyone else from doing it."

Nina was beginning to understand the Herculean task Scott was faced with. She didn't envy him. Her publicity ideas were going to make his job that much harder. "I hate to add to your problems…"

"Then don't." He grinned at her. "I won't be upset with you."

"Unfortunately, I had a brainstorm this afternoon and Miss E. and Lydia really like the idea."

"Hit me with it with both barrels between the eyes. Did you get a petulant tween pop star to do a concert here?"

"Not exactly." She found she couldn't meet his eyes. "I honestly like you way too much to do something like that."

"Then get it out."

"I came up with a theme for the New Year's Eve bash, Rio in Reno. And part of the allure for our event is going to be a jackpot going to one big winner."

Dread filled his eyes. "Go on."

"Ten million dollars, which will be on display in the casino. I was thinking the cashier's cage since it's already reinforced and secure."

"No," he said. "Hell, no. You are not putting ten million dollars on display."

Nina jumped into defensive mode. "Why ever not? It will bring a ton of people into the casino."

"That's insane." He ran a hand through his hair. "You're insane."

"It's not the worst thing I've ever been called." And she'd been called a lot of names over the years. "What's wrong with my idea?"

"Because a trillion million people are going to wonder how they can steal that ten million dollars. You're inviting trouble and I'll have to clean up the mess."

The waitress brought her food and iced tea. Nina took an experimental bite and decided the food tasted all right. Not great, but good enough to eat.

"We don't have to use the real thing, maybe pretend dollars. Just so people get an idea of what ten million would look like." Nina didn't really like that idea. People weren't going to come into the casino to look at pretend dollars. They wanted the real thing.

"Fake money would be even worse," Scott said. "It would still draw a criminal element because they'll be thinking the real thing is somewhere in the casino, they would just have to find it." He leaned his head back against the wall and banged it twice. "This is going to be a nightmare."

"You can hire extra security. Maybe a couple of armed guards who are with the money all the time."

Scott rubbed his forehead.

"I'm not doing this to you on purpose." The draw of a ten-million-dollar jackpot would put the Casa de Mariposa on the map. Miss E. really liked the idea, though Lydia had been a bit more reticent. "And Miss E. and Lydia are okay with it."

Scott sighed. "I'm not saying it's a bad idea or a good idea, but that it's a logistical nightmare."

Nina wanted to pat his hand, but didn't. "Life's a logistical nightmare."

He shook his head. "Let me think about. If I can't come up with a safe way of doing this, then it's off the table."

Not the answer Nina wanted, but she was grateful he was willing to consider it.

* * *

A commotion sounded at the door. Scott look up to find Anastasia Parrish standing in the entry, her purse slung over one shoulder and her dog's face peeking out. Oh no! Not her. Not here. Not now.

Irritated at the interruption, he scowled at Anastasia as she pranced across the room toward him. She wore a too-tight dress with stiletto heels that added a slinky element to her walk.

He'd been enjoying the verbal sparring with Nina. She didn't back down and he rather liked knowing she was so passionate about her job. Truth be known, he was really starting to like her. He liked every little thing about her, especially the way her dress clung to her curves and the bounce in her hair. He wasn't certain about the dog, but if she and the dog were a package deal, he could handle that. What he couldn't handle was Anastasia and her little dog.

"There you are, Scott." The woman grinned at him before turning to Nina, her smile dimming a little. "Nina Torres. I didn't expect to find you here." Her gaze moved rapidly back and forth between Nina and Scott.

"Anastasia Parrish." Nina stood and Anastasia gave Nina an air kiss. "What are you doing in Reno?"

Anastasia set her purse on the table and the tiny dog inside barked at Scott.

"Pets aren't allowed in the restaurant, Miss Parrish." Scott picked the purse up and handed it back to her.

"Don't be silly. Duchess isn't a pet. She's my emotional support dog. She even has a little sweater that says that." Anastasia's eyebrows rose.

"This is not negotiable," Scott said, trying to stay calm. "The health department has very strict rules about pets in a food service area."

"I'll take him to my room in a moment. Did you bring Kong?" Anastasia asked Nina.

"Of course. One of the owners has a daughter, and Maya is dog-sitting," Nina answered.

Anastasia clapped her hands. "Kong and Duchess need to have a play date."

Scott stood. Dogs! Playdates! Really? He stood with the idea of escorting Anastasia out of the restaurant. But she slid into the booth next to Nina.

"What are you doing here?" Anastasia asked Nina. "I thought you were in Los Angeles."

"Working. I'm doing promotions for the hotel. I assume you're here playing."

Anastasia gave Scott a come-hither look. "I'm trying to convince Scott to return to DC and work for Daddy." She giggled a little.

No. No way. Oh hell, no way. The last thing he wanted was to work for her father. Senator Parrish had his fingers in a couple of pies that had the possibility of turning into a sticky mess that could ruin careers. Scott had no desire to be anywhere near the senator when, or if, the meltdown happened.

Nina gave him a raised brow. He shook his head.

"Daddy was so disappointed when you told him you couldn't work on his new campaign," Anastasia continued to Nina.

A look appeared in Nina's eyes telling Scott she didn't want to work for "Daddy, " either.

Nina pushed her plate away. "Excuse me, but I have work to do. Scott, you will think about what I said."

Anastasia stood and let Nina get out. Then she slid back into the booth and batted her eyes at Scott.

"I'll get back to you," he said to Nina. He wasn't making any promises.

Nina tossed money on the table and left, her long-legged, enticing stride catching his gaze. She was hot, sexy and alluring. Scott wished he were going with her. He didn't want to be left alone with Anastasia.

She put a hand on his arm. "You are so tense, Scott. You need a cocktail." She snapped her fingers at the waitress hovering just out of range. "A peach margarita, please, and a martini for Scott."

The waitress looked at Scott. The last thing he needed was a drink. He shook his head.

"Have you ever thought," he said to Anastasia, "that the world isn't your oyster and you can't get everything you want because of who you are?"

"I can do things for you." She leaned toward him, the neck of her dress gaping slightly to show more of her cleavage. "I can open doors, introduce you to all the right people. You don't have to work here. You can be so much more. I want to help you attain your potential."

"I don't want your help and I don't need your help," Scott said, scowling. Anastasia wasn't used to having people say no to her.

She waved a hand. "This is a third-rate casino in Reno."

"If it's a third-rate casino in Reno, then why are you here? I'm sure the Hilton is more your style."

She batted her eyes at him. "I came to rescue you."

Like he needed rescuing. "From what?"

"Mediocrity," she said with a smug smile.

"You know nothing about how to win friends and influence people." Scott closed his laptop and gathered up the papers he'd been reading. He glanced at Barney the bookie's table, but Barney had slipped out while Scott's attention had been elsewhere. He'd deal with the man later, but now he needed to get as far away from Anastasia Parrish as possible.

Chapter 4

Nina liked the suite Miss E. has assigned to her. She'd set up an office in the dining alcove. Miss E. had even given her an assistant. Caroline Fairchild was Lydia's mother and though she had few skills, she knew how to organize. She'd mustered office supplies, a printer and a small cabinet on casters that could be moved out of sight if Nina wanted it that way.

Caroline was as fragile-looking as her daughter, but even Nina could see she had a core of steel.

Kong danced around Caroline's feet. Until a few minutes ago, Maya had been playing with him, but she had been picked up by Lydia for her riding lesson.

"This is the list of people I want you to start contacting." She handed Caroline a sheet of paper. "All their phone numbers are on my phone. I want you to call them and tell them you're my assistant and ask them what they're doing for New Year's Eve. If they have no plans, then tell them they're coming to Reno."

"And when they ask why?" Caroline asked.

"Because they're doing me a favor." She handed Caroline a second piece of paper. "These are the perks they can expect to receive. If they say no, don't pressure them."

Nina picked up her second phone and flipped through the contact list. She had her own list of personal friends she would call. Atomic MC was number one. Theo Nash was one of her favorite people. As Atomic MC he had a huge following and had built it all through the internet.

"Theo," she said.

"Baby girl, how are you doing?"

"I'm doing well, thank you. I haven't heard from you in a while. I hear you hosted a charity event for the Brotherhood Foundation at Madison Square Garden. What was the final take?"

"We tripled what we raised last year," Theo said. "I owe it all to you, baby girl. You are brilliant."

"Thank you."

"I owe you everything."

"How would you like to even the score?" Nina laughed.

"For you, anything."

"I think you and your family should come to Reno for New Year's Eve as guests of the Casa de Mariposa Hotel and Casino."

"Reno, as in not Las Vegas." He sounded cautious as though Reno were as far away as Mars.

"It's still in Nevada. And it's a hop, skip and a jump from Los Angeles."

"Isn't Reno Bobby Joe Watkins territory?"

"And he is next on my list of people to call." Country-Western singer Bobby Joe owed her a favor, too. She'd gotten him on *Singsation* as a judge and the exposure had revitalized his career.

In the background she could hear Caroline on the phone. Her tone was calm. Nina glanced at her and could see the oddest smile on her lips.

"I'll talk to my wife."

"I'll call Laynie. I'm booking her a free day at our brand-new spa and she'll absolutely adore the new shopping concourse." The shopping concourse wasn't new, but Kenzie was working on it.

"Okay, then." Theo disconnected.

"Do you really know all these people?" Caroline asked.

Nina put her phone down. "I've worked with most of them."

"How do you get into a job like this?"

"I fell into it. I'm the odd one in the Torres family."

"In what way are you 'odd'?" Caroline asked.

"I have no talent."

Caroline frowned. "But you're putting this celebration together so effortlessly."

"Not that." Nina waved her hand. "I have no musical talent in a family that has more than they know what to do with. I can't sing. I can't play an instrument. Although I can manage a pretty awesome samba, which would be okay if my brother wasn't the top choreographer for half the Broadway shows in New York. I have another brother who can play every instrument known to man including the kazoo. My sister writes music for every pop star. My dad is Manny Torres…"

"The jazz musician!" Caroline's eyes glowed.

"That would be him. My mother is Grace Torres. She's sung backup for just about every singer in the world."

"You must have had an interesting childhood."

"Never a dull moment. My passport was completely stamped by the time I was twelve."

"How exciting."

"You lived in New Orleans. How could you not have an exciting life?" she asked Caroline.

"I was so focused on getting out of poverty that I never let myself have any fun."

Nina hugged her. "That's about to change."

* * *

Scott sat at his desk, hunched over his laptop, staring at it without really seeing it. His mind was focused on the changes Nina had told him about.

A knock sounded at the door and Nina popped her head in. "You texted me about a problem."

"Come on in and sit." He pointed at an industrial-looking chair. His office was Spartan and small. His grandmother had tried to talk him into something larger and more comfortable, but Scott saw no need for anything other than this. He'd chosen a room next to the control center. It had made a few of the security guards uneasy, which was what Scott wanted.

Nina gave him an easy smile. "So what's wrong?" She wore a tight dress of pink and black, filled with a pattern that made him cross his eyes. She wore funky shoes that had hearts all over them. She was vibrant and alive.

He handed her a list of names with Atomic MC at the top. "He just made reservations for ten rooms."

She gazed at him curiously. "So what's the problem?"

"I can't have him and his gangsta thugs in this hotel."

She glanced at the list. "No gangstas on this list. His parents, his wife, their three children, a nanny, a personal assistant, a couple bodyguards and a snowboarding coach for his eldest son. His oldest son is a nationally ranked snowboarder. This kid has been racking up endorsements since he was ten. We might be able to do some business with his endorsement companies, who might pick up some of the tab for the party. If we play this right, this could be a great place for snowboarders." She handed the paper back to him. She whipped out her phone. "I have to text the concierge and set up a time to talk about snowboarding excursions."

"You know Celia already?" She'd been here two whole

days. Scott was completely amazed at how easily she'd inserted herself into everyone's lives.

"She's a doll. I'm surprised she's not on your go-to list." She sighed. "She knows everything about Reno and she loves to write. She's agreed to take over the blog from Eydie once it's set up and working properly."

Scott shook his head. All that energy she never seemed to lose made him feel tired. After every meeting with her, he wanted a nap. Actually, he wanted to take a nap with her. His thoughts shied away from that image.

She tapped at her iPhone quickly, her mouth tight with concentration and her eyes slightly narrowed. She crossed shapely legs as she stared at the phone and then her face lit up with a smile.

He couldn't help staring at her legs and her shoes. Women in DC were very conservative in their dress. The wild women wore navy blue with red shoes. Nina was as flamboyant in her dress as she was in personality. Something stirred in him. He sat back in his desk chair and studied her. She had jumped out of the chair to pace back and forth like a leopard on the prowl.

Kenzie told him after meeting Nina at the pool to *just get out of her way because it's painful when she runs over you.*

"I can start promoting the information that Atomic MC is going to be here."

"But he's…" For the most part, Scott disliked the negative connotations of rap music.

"Have you ever listened to him?" Nina demanded.

"No."

"His message is very positive."

Scott was going to need a lot of extra staff. More than he originally thought. He didn't trust the staff he had now. He needed to talk to his grandmother and Lydia. A good security staff cost a lot of money. The people he had now were mostly minimum-wage, cop wannabes with a powerful union on their side. He needed to talk to a lawyer, too.

She stopped pacing and leaned over his desk, her hands planted flat on the desktop. "You look a little stressed."

"Only a little."

"I know you have a lot of concerns and you need to tell me. You'd be amazed at what I can help you with."

"What do you know about security?"

"You'd be surprised. I can't have some celebrity dying facedown in a toilet. The publicity would ruin me and whoever I'm working for. How can I spin that for TMZ?"

"I want to talk about it, but not here."

"Oh, clandestine. I'm in," she gushed. She paused. "You like cars, don't you? Of course you do, you're a man. Let's go to the car museum. I'll bet you're a John Wayne fan. His Corvette is in the museum. And James Dean's car from *Rebel Without a Cause*."

How could he say no to an invitation like this? Scott was an avid John Wayne fan. He didn't advertise it because a lot of people thought it was silly. "Let me call my assistant and then we'll go." He glanced at the wall clock. "Lunch is on me."

"And we can work on your security worries." Nina grinned at him, holding out her hand.

He took her hand. Her skin was soft and smooth. A whiff of her perfume tickled at his nose. "I'll meet you in the lobby in fifteen minutes."

"I'll get my walking shoes on."

Nina ran to the elevator and punched the button to take her up to her suite. A man entered with her. He grinned at her.

"Going up," he said in a flirtatious manner. "I'm Gary, head of security."

For a second, Nina was confused. Wasn't Scott head of security? She tilted her head at him and his grin grew wider. He held out a hand and she noticed a small eagle's head tattooed on the back of it.

"Hello," she said. "I thought Mr. Russell is head of security."

"I'm second-in-command," he announced. His eyes darted up and down taking in her measure. "How about a drink later?"

"No, thank you." She didn't like him.

"Another time then." The doors opened on the fifth floor. He stepped out, then turned to salute her as the doors closed again, taking her to her floor.

Inside her suite, Nina kicked off her shoes and ran into the bedroom to grab a pair of shoes more conducive to walking. They were half the height of her normal shoes, but the daisies sprinkled around the outside always made her feel like she was walking through a field of flowers. She grabbed her purse just as her phone received a text from Carl.

Where are you?

What did Carl want? She read the text and could hear his voice in her mind whining. "If you hadn't believed your own press, you'd have an Academy Award by now," she said to the phone as though she were talking directly to him. "You're an egotistical boy-man." Her mother had told her on the day of her wedding that God was not done cooking Carl and was she certain she wanted to take on this project.

Nina remembered the words, but her real thoughts had been on her Vera Wang wedding dress and what she thought was love for Carl. She'd brushed her mother's words aside and married Carl anyway. She should have listened. Hindsight was always twenty-twenty.

She put the phone in her purse. She'd answer him later.

The elevator deposited her in the lobby. The second she stepped out of the elevator, she spotted him. Carl. What the hell was he doing here? How did he find her?

Carl stood at the reception desk signing something. Tiffani with an *i* stood at his side, her blond hair hanging in luxurious waves down her back. Her black dress was too tight and the neckline much too low.

"I recognize that look of panic on your face," Celia Grantham said. As concierge, Celia was very conscious of the hotel's image and was dressed conservatively in a beige skirt and dark brown blazer with a light yellow silk blouse. "What do you need?"

"Ex-husband at three o'clock."

Celia glanced at the desk. "The one with the bimbo!"

"That's the one."

"Where do you need to go?"

"I'm meeting Scott at the front door."

"Got ya." Celia pulled her phone of her pocket and texted someone. "Thirty seconds."

Celia's assistant appeared at the desk and a look of adoration filled her face. She started fawning over Carl and Tiffani and drawing them toward the concierge's desk so their backs were to Nina.

"You just earned yourself a little reward, Celia."

Celia looked surprised and then pleased. "Thank you. There's no need for a reward. This is my job."

"You look like a Prada girl." Nina could get a couple of purses for free. She'd send one to Celia and one to her assistant.

Celia nodded at Nina who almost leaped at the front door just as Scott appeared in the arch that led to the casino. He saw her, his eyebrows arching up as she grabbed him and pulled him out the door.

"What's wrong?"

"Just keep walking. The bane of my existence just arrived." She hustled him toward the parking lot.

"And that would be?"

She signed. "The ex-husband and his little piece of bunny fluff."

Scott unlocked his black SUV, opened the passenger door and helped Nina in. The hem of her dress rose up to midthigh as she hopped inside. She repressed a chuckle at the look on Scott's face. Then she demurely tugged her dress down.

"Do you want to talk about it?" he asked after starting the SUV and putting it into gear.

"Why would you be interested in my personal life?" And did she want to talk about Carl to the man she was interested in?

"In the army we had to bond quickly in order to protect each other."

Nina stared at him. He was flirting with her. She liked being flirted with. She buckled her seatbelt and settled back against the cushion. "My story is a sad, but typical, Hollywood tale."

"Okay." He turned out of the parking lot and merged into traffic.

"My husband decided he didn't need me anymore and traded me in for a shiny new model. He thought his career could survive without me because he was established. And now he wants me back. His career stalled because he didn't understand how fickle Hollywood is. And I'm not quite sure, but I got the impression he wanted to start cheating on his present squeeze with his old one. Me."

Scott's eyebrows rose. "Carl should run for a political office. He'd fit right in."

Nina burst out laughing.

"What are you going to do?"

"Avoid him," she replied. The hotel was big, the casino bigger. Carl was easily distracted and he did like to gamble. Not a lot, but enough to keep his mind occupied. She pulled out her phone. "I need to send a text to Celia to steer him toward the blackjack table. The casino might as well make some money off him."

"You're bad, Nina."

She tilted her head at him. "In a good way. Right?"

"I didn't know there's a good way to be bad." Scott gave her a side glance, amusement on his face.

"There's always a good way to be bad, or at least a way to spin it."

He turned onto the highway. "So tell me. How did you get into doing what you do? Though I'm not certain what it is you do."

"Sometimes, it's hard to explain. But I try to make people, places and things famous." Her first big excursion into downtown Reno was eye-opening. She could fall in love with it.

"And how did you get into that as a career?"

"I majored in business at UCLA because I thought that was what I really wanted to do, but business wasn't fun. I wanted to do something fun. I discovered I was more creative in public relations and media then I would ever be in business. My parents started their restaurant when I was eleven. They wanted something more stable so they didn't have to be on the road all the time. And the logistics of having seven children made the whole task doubly difficult. Even though their educations were in completely different areas, they intuitively understood what people wanted and understood how to give it to them. All I did was study my parents and it was a great springboard to start my own business." And waitressing in the restaurant gave her untold contacts.

Kenzie had always known what she wanted to do and never deviated from her goal, but Nina hadn't been so focused. Her brothers and sister had also known what they wanted to accomplish. Nina had floundered for a bit until she realized she had a talent for creating buzz.

"My first job was this tiny mom-and-pop sushi place. Mr. and Mrs. Takada were the nicest people, but Sushi Joe's wasn't going well…"

"There's a Sushi Joe's in DC. I've eaten there."

"Was the food good?"

"Yeah."

"They have the Nina Roll."

Scott shook his head. "How did you propel them to national prominence?"

"I had this idea of hiring a down-and-out actor who used to come to my parents' place and I had a firestorm of a promotional idea, threw together a video highlighting Sushi Joe's and used the actor as the spokesperson. Sushi Joe's took off and so did the actor's career. I relaunched two careers for the price of one." Douglas Jameson had shown his gratitude by steering other clients to her. By the time she graduated from UCLA she'd already had a growing business. "I'm a schmoozer."

"I noticed that about you."

The drive to the museum was quick, but in the short span of time, Nina was deeply conscious of the man next to her. She found the subtle scent of his aftershave attractive. Despite the depth of seriousness he projected, she sensed a more sensitive side. She would just have to find a way to bring it out.

Scott found a place to park. They stepped out into the afternoon heat.

"Ninety-five percent of my job is a handshake or an air kiss," she said, tucking her hand around his elbow. The feel of hard muscles beneath her fingers sent a shiver through her as they walked up to the entrance.

"They have events here." Nina read a sign next to the ticket booth. "We should have something here. Men like cars, it shouldn't be too hard to get them in the door so they can drool over these classics."

Scott paid for two tickets. They wandered through the various rooms. Scott stopped to pet a Corvette.

"You're looking a little glazed over." Nina was enjoying the practiced nonchalance as he pretended to be so casual about a car he was definitely lusting over.

He patted the Corvette again. "This is one of the best moments ever. This is John Wayne's Corvette."

Nina gave the car a critical look. "He was a big man. How did he fit in that little car?"

"I'd make myself fit in this car." Awe showed in his tone and face.

"I feel the same way about fashion. When you order couture, you don't alter it to fit you—you alter yourself to fit into it."

They meandered through another room that was made to look like a turn-of-the-century street with early nine-teenth-century cars parked at the curb. Another area contained a theater marquee with *Gone with the Wind* being advertised. The Duesenberg parked in front of it had been owned by Sammy Davis, Jr.

While Scott drooled over the cars, Nina found herself attracted to the displays of vintage clothing. She was particularly enchanted with the children's pedal cars from the 1920s to the 1960s. The little cars looked like fun and she could imagine tooling around the cul-de-sac where her parents lived.

Caught up in the spirit of the exhibits, Nina realized she had to host an event here. It would be a challenge to schedule, with it being so late in the year, but she could talk her way into anything.

When Scott and Nina left the auto museum to have dinner at a restaurant a few blocks from the museum, he was still in raptures over the cars. Having Nina with him today had made the visit more than fun.

The restaurant was tiny with barely a dozen tables squeezed between a row of glass windows and a snack bar. The interior was a cheerful yellow and white with the waitresses in matching yellow-and-white uniforms. His brother, Hunter, had brought him when they'd been on some errands and Scott had truly enjoyed the family-style fare.

They sat at a table against the window. Scott wondered if he'd done the right thing in bringing Nina here. She didn't quite fit in, with her fashionable dress and weird daisy shoes. She was the kind of woman who needed to be seen.

A gum-snapping waitress slapped menus on the table covered in large square sheets of white paper. When diners were done, the paper was scooped up to reveal a clean one underneath. Easy-care dining.

"Ooh, meat loaf. I'm in," she said after scanning the plastic-coated menu with bent corners. "I haven't had meat loaf in ages."

"Meat loaf! I just don't picture you as a meat loaf kind of girl." He liked that she ate. And that she appreciated regular-people food. Nina was turning out to be quite a pleasant surprise. Normally he didn't like surprises but he certainly found himself liking her.

"Meat loaf is comfort food. And I don't always have the time to cook for myself, but if I did I'd eat meat loaf five days a week."

"Your life is that stressful?"

"Not stress-stress, but fun stress."

"There's a difference?" She was a curious mix of playfulness and seriousness. He found his thoughts straying to her too much during the course of a day. When he was on a job, he didn't like being so easily distracted—and Nina was definitely distracting him.

"My stress normally involves the people I have to deal with. They think that if someone is wearing the wrong bracelet with a particular type of dress, the world is going to come to an end. While that's truly funny, it's still stressful."

"And this is coming from the woman who looks like— and I am a man, so don't tell anyone I know this—she's straight out of the pages of *Vogue* magazine."

She laughed. "I won't tell anyone, except for maybe Kenzie…your grandmother…your brothers. But I won't tell anyone else. How does a big, tough guy like you know about fashion?"

She now had leverage on him, but it didn't make him nervous; it excited him. "There's a lot of downtime in security work. And sometimes the reading material is thin."

"So in other words, if you run security on upper-class divas, *Vogue* is all you have to read?"

"And *Essence, Marie Claire*, and on occasion, *Teen* magazine. I wish they spotlighted guns and ammo, but they only use them as props."

Their conversation was interrupted when the waitress returned to take their orders.

"You have a smartphone," Nina said once the waitress left their table. "You can get reading material on that."

"Smartphones take a lot of power and I never know when I might have to make an emergency call to someone's hairdresser." And he'd been forced into doing exactly that more than once for Anastasia.

"You sound like you really didn't enjoy being a bodyguard." She sipped her iced tea after swirling two teaspoons of sugar into it. He'd already noticed she liked sweet drinks.

"I love it. I just don't love the people I sometimes had to work for."

"Can you give me some detail?" She leaned her elbows on the table, leaning toward him, her eyes directly on his. "Start with Anastasia Parrish."

He almost choked. She looked completely captivated. Damn, that was sexy. "I can't talk directly, but I can give you examples. A lot of people want to treat their bodyguards as their personal go-to staff. How can I protect someone if they insist I walk the dog or fix a martini? I refuse to be an errand boy and have a clause written into my contracts that I do not provide any services other than security. I've had clients who felt I needed to discipline their children. No disciplining children, no doggy day care, no bartending."

"They really wanted you to walk the dog."

"I'm sure some stalker was out there planning how to take out Fido, despite the fact that Daddy was a high-ranking member of some influential committee and the theft of a dog was going to influence a vote."

"I'd give up a lot to save Kong."

"My favorite client was a high-ranking official who wanted to bring his family along on a tour of Iraq and Afghanistan. Thought it would be a fun family vacation.

He asked me if I knew where to purchase Kevlar for an eight-year-old." That had been a nightmare for Scott. He'd flatly refused to allow the senator's family to accompany him. The senator had thrown a tantrum, which totally disgusted Scott and he'd refused to work for him after that. He was constantly amazed at the number of times people voted over and over again for politicians who were so obviously incompetent.

The waitress brought their food. Scott had ordered a sirloin with baked potatoes and no vegetables. He was amused that Nina's meat loaf had vegetables and no potatoes. The waitress refilled their iced teas and left them to their food.

Nina took a tentative bite of her meat loaf and suddenly forked a large chunk into her mouth. "This is absolutely delicious. The chef is going to be my future ex-husband. And I have to bring my father here."

"And when my brother Donovan shows up, this is going to be our first meal the second he gets his luggage. Your father likes food?"

Nina didn't answer. She was too busy eating. And from the look of total adoration on her face, this tiny place was going to be one of her favorites, too.

"My father," she said, "is the odd man out in his family. He broke away from five generations of restaurateurs to be a musician. And the irony is, he ended up owning a restaurant eventually. He discovered that he loved cooking as much as he loved music and that he could be both." She sipped her tea and ate a little more meat loaf. "You do know you and I are going to find common ground and make Casa de Mariposa the finest resort in the whole world, don't you?"

The way she smiled at him made him want to give her

everything. "I'm willing to meet you halfway." His steak was delicious. Cooked medium rare just the way he liked it.

"Said with the conviction of a leaf in a hurricane," she said between bites.

"What the hell does that mean?"

"I'm not sure. It just popped into my head and sounded good."

The way she changed subjects, moved from one thought to another, was not only confusing, but charming in a way. He had to stay on his toes around her. The more time he spent with her, the more he realized why she was so good at her job. She was flexible and her zigzag way of thinking was probably the reason she was so good at multitasking. He'd never been good at that. When he took a job, he started with step one and followed each step until the job was concluded. He planned for contingencies, but knew that all the proper planning beforehand would result in an instinctive response if he faced something out of the ordinary.

"You're thinking so hard, I can almost hear you." Nina had finished her food and sat back in the chair looking completely satisfied, like a woman who'd just had the best sex ever.

That was way too sexy for his own good. He was going to have to watch himself around her. Nina was lethal. "You look content," he said.

"I am. That was the best meat loaf I've ever had. Just the right amount of seasoning to give it a delightful taste and just enough of other underlying flavors to make it feel like it just came out of grandma's kitchen. We have to come back."

Scott definitely agreed. Before he could respond, his phone rang.

"We have a problem here at the hotel," Celia Grantham

said when he answered the call. "Some teenagers are causing trouble. Your people aren't handling the situation."

"I'll be there in twenty minutes." He disconnected and raised a hand for the bill. "We're out of here," he told Nina as he handed money to the waitress.

"What's wrong?"

"Trouble at the hotel."

Chapter 5

The loud sounds of a party reached Scott through the elevator before the doors even opened. The penthouse floor had four suites along with the presidential suite and the one Scott wanted was farthest from the elevator. The elevator doors opened and Scott emerged.

Gary White and Celia Grantham waited in the hallway. She looked angry and worried.

Two more guards waited farther down the hall and Belle Sampson, the only female on Scott's staff, stood next to the door. She looked relieved when Scott nodded at her.

"We got the party quieted down," she said, "but the real problem is most of the kids are underage and the beer is flowing. That's why I called you."

"We felt you needed to be the one to handle this," Gary added. "You're the boss and there are a couple VIP kids inside."

Scott opened the door to the suite. Two dozen teens, many carrying beer cans, crowded the living room, dancing and yelling. Scott pulled the plug on the stereo and the music abruptly ended. A few teens kept dancing, but those nearest Scott looked confused as they came to a stop.

"Hey." A boy who looked to be maybe eighteen approached. He had blond hair cut close to his head and wore leather pants pulled down around his thighs and white boxer shorts underneath. His T-shirt, with a Tyrannosaurus rex silk-screened on the front, was too baggy for his slender frame, and the red baseball cap, positioned backward on his head, told Scott he was nothing more than gangsta lite. "What do you think you're doing? Turn the music back on."

Anastasia sidled up to Scott. Seeing her, Scott immediately understood why Celia insisted he be called. She wore a skin-tight black dress revealing too much cleavage. "Do you know who this is?" Her voice held a breathless quality. "That's T-Rex, the rapper. You're spoiling the best party I've been to in ages."

Even Scott had heard about the legendary exploits of the underage singer. He turned to Gary. "Start checking IDs. Have the under twenty-ones sit in that bedroom there, and start calling their parents. Anyone gives you trouble, cuff them."

A couple kids yelled at Scott, but he turned on them, a fierce look on his face. They subsided to angry mutters as Gary and Belle spread out and started checking IDs. A few girls sidled toward the open door, but Scott stepped in front of them and gestured at an empty sofa.

"I don't know who you think you are," T-Rex snapped. "I want to talk to the owner."

Scott whipped out his cell phone. "I'll call my grandmother."

T-Rex just stared at him.

Scott's eyebrows rose. "Nothing to say, son?"

T-Rex muttered under his breath. Belle was speaking to several girls who shook their heads emphatically. She herded them to the second bedroom.

Anastasia put a hand on Scott's arm. "Come on. We're just having fun."

"You realize," Scott said, "you are over twenty-one at

a party with underage teens drinking beer. You do realize you can be charged with contributing to the delinquency of a minor times the number of minors." He looked around. "I've eyeballed twenty-two so far."

Anastasia frowned. "It's a little party."

"A loud, little party at two in the afternoon on Saturday."

"This is a hotel. We're supposed to have fun." She tilted her head coyly and gave him a fluttering sidelong glance.

"Not with underage kids and alcohol."

"You know my daddy can get me out of any trouble."

"I know," Scott replied. "But how quiet can this be kept? I don't think your father's reach extends all the way to Reno, Nevada."

Her eyes narrowed. "Are you threatening me?"

"I'm making a promise. This is Saturday afternoon and I can have you arrested and with the courts closed for the weekend, you won't be arraigned until Monday morning. Think you can spend the next forty or so hours in jail?"

Anastasia turned white. "You wouldn't."

"I would. And I will personally call your father to tell him and apprise him of the situation. And after I talk to him, one of two things is going to happen. Either he'll drop everything and get out here to get his little girl out of jail and run the risk of looking bad to his constituents for thinking his daughter gets special treatment, or he will leave you to rot in jail. This is an election year and he's running a 'tough on crime' platform. Your father may love you, but he will eat his own young to stay in office." And another reason why he refused to work for the senator. "So being as we're in Reno, you can take a risk, or be as sweet as pie by cooperating with me and the Reno PD."

She crossed her arms over her breasts, a challenge in her eyes. "Go ahead. Call him. I don't care."

He pulled his phone out of his pocket and smiled. "I have him on speed dial." He paused, watching her out of the side of his eyes.

Indecision warred with anger on her face. She didn't totally believe him. He flipped through his contact list, lifted the phone to show her father's photo and his private cell phone number with his thumb poised over the call icon.

She grabbed at his phone. "Okay. Okay."

He pointed at the sofa. "Sit," he ordered. He doubted she knew any of these kids except for T-Rex, but Scott never left a stone unturned.

Scott spent the rest of the afternoon dealing with the situation. By the time the last parent picked up their errant child, he was almost too tired to go back to his office. When he finally got back to his office, Scott found Belle waiting for him.

Belle Sampson was an attractive woman in her late thirties with light brown hair with reddish highlights and green eyes. He'd read her file and knew she'd been a cop in Chicago before taking the job in Reno. Her reason was that she was tired of cold and snow and wanted warmth and sunshine. Scott suspected that wasn't the real reason, but hadn't pressed her for a better answer. If she wanted to confide in him, it would be on her terms. He was a stranger and hadn't proved yet that he'd earned her trust.

"That was a lot of beer and assorted alcohol," he said. "I checked the room records and the hotel bar delivered it all and no one asked for an ID and T-Rex paid for everything with his manager's credit card."

Disgust showed on her face. "Someone got paid off."

Scott already suspected that. "Who? The bartender?"

She shrugged. "Possibly."

Since the Reno PD already had a sting operation going

on in the bar, he would just notify the police liaison he was working with about the situation and let them handle it.

For the first time since he'd agreed to take over the job, he had someone he thought he could trust. But how could he earn Belle's trust?

"You were very good dealing with the girls at the party."

"I worked juvenile detention for a couple years. Usually I dealt with the hardcore cases. These kids were being naughty, but underneath they're pretty good. They just wanted to have fun."

"There's no fun on my watch."

She chuckled. "You do realize you work in a casino. *Fun* is the buzzword on the casino floor."

"So I've been told." He leaned back in his chair. "According to your file, you were passed over for two promotions. Care to tell me why?"

"I'm not part of the fun crowd."

"Who's the fun crowd?"

"I have my suspicions."

"I'd like to schedule a more in-depth meeting to talk about your future at the Casa de Mariposa."

She tilted her head and studied him. "I'd like that, but not here. Off-site."

He nodded. "I know just the place. I'll call you and leave the name on your voice mail."

She left and he stared at the closed door, thinking hard. A second later a knock sounded and Nina walked in.

"You had a busy day. A morning of fun and an afternoon of work." She sat down.

"What can I help you with?"

"I'm here to do some damage control."

He frowned. "What do you mean?"

"Anastasia called in a panic. She's picturing herself in an orange jumpsuit with no spa service."

"The horror," Scott said with a wry grin

Nina rolled her eyes. "No kidding. I've seen her without makeup."

"So have I."

She chuckled. "Paint by numbers, right?"

He wanted to laugh, but held it in. He always found himself pushing his control around her. This woman made him feel reckless and out of control, but the worst part of it was that he was okay with it.

"Come on," Nina said. "That was funny."

He shook his head and let the laughter out. "So what kind of spin did you have in mind?"

"The last thing we need is for Anastasia to go to the press, mentioning this hotel and police brutality in the same sentence." She paused.

"But," Scott coaxed.

"I had a hard time explaining to her that you aren't the police."

"Do you want me to brush her involvement underneath the rug?"

Nina shook her head emphatically and gave him a sexy little pout. "Heavens, no. That would be breaking the law. I don't have a lot of rules, but I only break them when I'm the one having fun."

"So," Scott said carefully, "you want me to do what?" Because he would pretty much do anything to get her to smile at him. Weak, man, weak.

"Make her the hero of this tale."

He felt his face scrunching up.

"That is not an attractive look for you," Nina said batting her eyelashes at him.

Oh, she had his number all right. "Right now in my head, I'm going over the sentence where you said 'make her the hero of this tale.' How do I do that?"

"She tried to get them to toss the beers and replace them with soda."

"Is that what she said to you?"

"We're co-authors of the tale."

"I'm not lying for her, but I will tell the press she was trying to calm things down since she is registered in the suite next door and knew about T-Rex's reputation."

She waved her hands at him. "Allude all you need to."

"What she really wants is for me not to call her father."

"That would be considered a kindness on your part. Anastasia thanks you and has offered her services in helping me promote the hotel."

Oh, great. Politics added into the equation.

"Then I can count on your cooperation?"

"Does anyone ever tell you no?" This woman fascinated him. She had a way of getting whatever she wanted without being obvious. And yet he didn't feel trapped or defensive.

"My mother, when she's promoting my moral well-being." Nina laughed. "Which reminds me, I have to get down to the lobby. My parents said they'd be here around five or five-thirty and I want to be there to greet them."

"Me, too." Scott rose. He could deal with things later. He was too curious about Nina's parents to waste the moment to meet them.

The moment her parents entered the lobby, the air changed with a wave of energy that almost knocked Nina off her feet. Her father's boisterous laugh turned heads, and her mother's delicate beauty almost caused a riot. Half the people in the lobby recognized them for their music and started to converge on them as they walked to the reception desk to check in.

Nina was deeply proud of her parents. They'd accomplished so much and their generosity touched so many people.

"Nina," her mother yelled.

Her father grabbed her up in a huge hug and half swung her around. "Nina." He planted a huge kiss on her cheek before setting her back on her feet. "It's been forever since I last saw you."

Nina laughed. "Five days' worth of forever."

He looked around and grinned at the guests who watched him. He swung his arms out and yelled, "This is my daughter."

Nina caught Scott grinning at her. "You'll have to forgive them. They are unusually subdued today. Mom, Dad, this is Scott Russell, Miss E.'s grandson."

Her father pushed a hand out and grasped Scott's in a firm shake. Her mother kissed him on the cheek. Scott greeted them, "Good evening, Mrs. Torres, Mr. Torres."

"I don't know who Mr. Torres is." Her father slapped Scott on the shoulder. "We are not so formal. Manny. Grace."

"Let's get you checked in and up to your suite." Nina herded them toward the reception desk.

"I'm starving," Manny said.

Grace nudged him. "What else is new?"

Nina laughed. Her parents gave her such joy she could hardly contain it. No one could be sad or melancholy around them. They had no time for anything but happiness and joy.

Thirty minutes later they all stood in the half-empty restaurant. No matter how empty a room could be, her parents made if feel crowded.

Celia had arranged for Manny to tour the kitchen before they ate. Nina tried not to think what would happen when he got there. Her father had a habit of taking over and angering kitchen staff.

The kitchen was huge since its job was to feed the people of two restaurants, the bar and the snack shop as well as provide room service meals. Manny walked around, looking at each station, either nodding approval or frowning. Nina stood to the side knowing that at some point something would happen.

A shout sounded. She twisted to see the line chef rushing to a sink to run water over a red burn on his wrist. The head chef looked up from his station, frowning. "Get back to work, Rodriguez. You don't have time to be burned."

Manny walked quickly to the station and turned to the head chef. "The flame is too high. No wonder the boy is burned."

The head chef just glared at Manny. "You are in my kitchen and I do not take orders from you."

Nina grabbed the first aid kit. At first glance it didn't look too bad, but she ordered him to the infirmary to have it checked out.

"I cannot leave." Fear stood out on his face. "I need to get back to work."

Scott smiled at him. "Get your wrist checked out first. I'll handle this."

The young man gratefully slipped away.

Manny glanced around. "Look at these young people," he said to the chef. "They are afraid of you."

"That's the way I like it," the head chef snarled, turning back to his station.

"You cannot cook with fear. Food is about love, joy, passion. You cannot make these people afraid. No wonder the restaurant is almost empty."

"Dad," Nina said soothingly.

"Manny, this is not your kitchen." Her mother put a hand on his arm.

"Listen to the old broad," the chef said with an oily smile.

"*Mi canário*," Manny said with a gentle smile at Grace and Nina. "I will handle this."

Celia looked poised to take flight. Nina gave the woman a nod, letting her know she could leave and that she and Scott could handle the situation.

Scott stood next to Manny, looking intimidating. Which was really hot. Wow, she was never into big sexy commando men. What had she been missing?

"First, I will apologize for storming into your kitchen. If you choose to run it like a cheap, petty dictator, that is your right."

The chef's face grew into a huge scowl.

"Second," Manny continued, "you will apologize to my wife. She is a lady. For some reason she felt the need to defend you and your barbaric methods."

No, no, no, Nina thought. Her father cloaked his diplomacy in sarcasm and insults.

"Thirdly," Manny went on without taking a breath, "you will apologize to your workers for being an insensitive, uncaring leader."

Waitstaff gathered by the door and the under-chefs stood at their stations trying to make themselves look small. Nina knew the moment her father left the kitchen, the chef would take his humiliation out on them.

"Well," the chef said, his scowl deepening. He stalked up to Scott. "You can tell your grandmother I quit." He took off his apron and his toque, flinging them on the floor. He stomped out of the kitchen and Nina tried not to cringe at the scene that would shortly be going down in Human Resources.

Without missing a beat, Manny said. "Good." He snapped his fingers. "Someone get me an apron."

"Dad," Nina said," you can't cook here. This is Miss E.'s hotel."

"Nonsense," he replied. "I'm a guest chef. Miss E. will allow it. She likes my cooking." An under-chef handed him a clean apron and a toque for his head and Manny spun around to take in everything. "I will cook and then we will clean. Then I will teach you all how to cook with passion."

Nina pushed Scott and her mother out of the kitchen. Once her father's mind was made up there was no changing it.

A crowd of diners had gathered at the swinging doors leading to the kitchen. Nina shoved through them, opening a channel for her mother. Scott made soothing sounds and urged the diners back to their tables.

"Is he always like this?" Scott asked when they sat at their booth.

"He gets testy when people don't take care of their workers," Grace said with a shrug. "Or when people don't cook with joy, love and passion."

Scott's face held nothing but amusement and Nina started to relax. Most men found her father intimidating. Scott wasn't put off. "And he has no tolerance for poorly cooked anything."

Scott took out his phone. "I should probably let my grandmother know what happened."

Nina saw a movement in the corner of her eye and saw Miss E. entering the restaurant. "I think she already found out."

Miss E. stopped at their table.

"I'm sorry, Miss E.," Grace began.

"I'm not," Miss E. said, scooting in next to her grandson. "I didn't like the man anyway. Now that Manny is in the kitchen, I can eat here."

"You wanted to get rid of him?" Scott said curiously.

Miss E. laughed. "The minute I knew Manny was coming, I knew he'd get rid of him for me."

Nina burst out laughing. "So that's why you wanted me to invite them."

Miss E. waved her hand. "Grace, you and Manny are two of my favorite people."

Grace's eyes twinkled. "You are a devious woman, Miss E."

Miss E. bowed her head gracefully. "Of course."

"What's going to happen when Donovan arrives?" Scott looked a little confused.

Nina wanted to comfort him. Her parents were a lot to take in and things happened around them very quickly.

"Don't worry about Donovan," Miss E. said. "He and Manny will get along just fine." She raised her hand to signal the waitress who rushed over as quickly as she could.

Grace reached out to Miss E. and gripped her hand. "While Manny is getting the kitchen in shape, I will be thinking about music. Miss E., this place is just too quiet."

"And you will make it noisy."

Grace gave a catlike grin. "I will make it sing."

After dinner, Nina found Kenzie in the gift shop.

"All this ticky-tacky stuff has to go," Kenzie told the manager. "Put it on sale. I don't care how you get rid of it."

The manager, a woman who looked to be around twenty-five, pressed her lips tightly together. She wore a tag with the name Zoe embossed on it. "Miss Russell, I've been the manager here for a year and I know how to improve sales."

Kenzie shook her head. "I'm going to get beautiful things for this shop and the clothing shop."

Nina looked around, finding she agreed with Kenzie.

"First, I'm leaving for Brazil tomorrow. I'll be in Rio. I'll be looking for special things for our Rio-in-Reno celebration. I want classy, beautiful. While I'm gone, I want you to look at things and ask yourself, is this classy, sophisticated, chic? And stop thinking cheap and start thinking boutique."

The girl's face turned mutinous. "But Miss Russell… this is not the classiest hotel."

Kenzie just smiled. "But it will be. We're going to make the Bellagio look like a no-tell motel. So think elegance, think beauty, think class."

Zoe looked around, her eyes squinting. "The fixtures have to go, then."

"Collect ideas and put them in a folder and I will go over them with you when I return."

Kenzie looped her arm through Nina's. "Let's go before she thinks about it too hard."

"You're going to make her into a little mini-me, aren't you?" Nina said with a laugh.

Kenzie glanced back at Zoe who stood in the center of the store, eyes squinting and thinking hard. "When I'm done with that girl, she'll be able to get a job with any fashion house in Paris, but she won't. She'll stay with me forever. So what are your plans for the evening?"

"Do I detect a suspicious undertone in your question?"

"I have no idea what you mean." Kenzie tried for an innocent look, but couldn't quite pull it off.

"You're being nosy. Maybe I'm going up to my suite, opening a bottle of wine and putting my feet up. It's been quite a day."

"Are you going to be doing it alone?"

Nina shrugged. "I haven't gotten that far into my planning."

"You should invite Scott."

Nina stared at her friend suspiciously. Did her friend know that she was attracted to her brother? Damn that woman—too smart for her own good. "Why should I invite Scott to my *quality alone* time?"

"So he can have quality alone time with you." The look of innocence just didn't work on Kenzie's face.

"And if I want to be alone…" Nina's voice trailed off. "It's been a stressful afternoon."

"I'm sure he's stressed out, too."

Nina stopped and jerked Kenzie to a stop next to her. "I have known you for how many years? You have never attempted to set me up with one of your brothers. Why are you doing it now?"

"You never met Scott before."

And Scott was making her a bit nutty. "But Donovan and Hunter are perfectly good men."

"Of course they are," Kenzie conceded. "But not perfectly good men for you."

"So you're offering me the uptight, anal-retentive, stiff-necked brother."

"He is all those things, but not in a bad way. He could use a woman who is fun-loving, passionate and impulsive just like you."

Nina's eyes narrowed to slits. She wasn't that good. "I don't need you to help me find a guy."

"Your last experiment was Carl. You need my help."

Nina flinched. "Ouch."

Kenzie nudged her good-naturedly. "We're friends. Be honest. The only good thing you got out of the marriage was that dog."

"Stop being so honest with me." Mention of Kong reminded her she'd barely seen him all day. She hoped he hadn't worn Maya out. Lydia's daughter had taken the responsibility of taking care of a dog very seriously. She was trying to impress her mother. "Okay, I'll call your brother and ask him if he wants some quality alone time with me. I'm sure he'll say no. He thinks I make him crazy."

Kenzie gave her an odd look. "I hope you do. Call him, or I will."

Nina sighed. It's not like she didn't want to spend time alone with him. "All right. All right. I'll call him. When did you become such a bully?"

"I've always been a bully, but it's hard to outshine your parents."

Nina started laughing. "Have a good trip to Brazil."

Kenzie headed back into the gift shop while Nina pulled her phone out of her pocket to call Scott. He agreed to meet her in her suite and said he'd bring the wine. Nina let out a low sigh.

Scott knocked on Nina's door, a bottle of chilled Chardonnay in one hand and a bottle of merlot in a bag dangling from his arm. She opened the door and he smiled. She'd changed into casual jeans and a loose T-shirt. Gold hoops hung from her ears and she'd swept her hair back from her face and secured it with multicolored barrettes dotted with rhinestones that caught the fading sunlight with tiny little flashes. Something about her glowed. She was the most beautiful woman he had seen in a long time. She was so alive and vibrant he had to stop himself from touching her. They worked together and she was his sister's friend. Hell, she wasn't going to be around long enough for him to see if they could get something started.

"Come on in." She stood aside to let him into the suite.

Her suite was a carbon copy of all the others, though smaller. The living area consisted of a sofa and two over-stuffed chairs upholstered in yellows and oranges. A small dining room and kitchen overlooked the pool. The sounds of late-night swimming, splashing and laughter filled the night. A bedroom and bath opened off the living room. She'd opened the sliding doors to the balcony and a light evening breeze filtered in.

"I don't think I have a bottle opener. At least I couldn't find one," she said after an approving look at the two bottles.

"Never leave home without one." He held up a Swiss Army knife and headed for the kitchen. She'd set out two wineglasses on the counter and a small plate of assorted truffles. "Chardonnay or merlot?"

"Chardonnay."

Glad that she was pleased, he opened the bottle and poured two glasses of wine. He handed one to her, and she wandered out onto the balcony. He followed her to lean against the railing. She set the plate of truffles down on a glass-topped table and stood next to him sipping her wine. Below them, underwater lights lit up the swimming pool. A group of adults had commandeered the spa and sat in it laughing and talking while kids jumped off the diving board trying to make large splashes.

"I saw on Anastasia's Twitter feed that she was partying with T-Rex. She posted photos on Instagram." Nina frowned slightly. "That girl cannot keep quiet about anything."

"She made it difficult to make her the hero in this."

Nina shook her head. "Yeah, it's hard to spin stupid."

The woman had a wicked sense of humor. "Some of the kids posted photos and a few parents were annoyed to have the world know their underage kids were partying with an underage celebrity who's been in rehab twice."

"My question is where were they while their children were partying?"

Scott just shrugged. "It's easy to sneak out."

"Spoken by someone who did?"

He grinned. "I had an adventure or two."

She tilted her head to study him. "I have a hard time seeing you getting out from under Miss E.'s thumb."

He laughed. He wasn't about to tell her some of his adolescent misadventures, although he knew it would please her. "It took planning, but every once in a while, I got a sweet taste of freedom." Donovan was his coconspirator. Hunter had been too serious to enjoy challenging authority. "As long as Donovan and I escaped Kenzie's notice, we managed."

"If you'd taken her with you, you might have gotten away with a few more things."

"If she'd known ahead of time of our plans, she'd run right to Miss E. We called her Kenzie the Informer."

"Kenzie only told on you when you didn't take her along. You seriously misjudged your sister. She had to go all the way to Paris for her misadventures."

"What?"

She leaned toward him, her face full of mischief. "I'll never tell, because they included me."

The Chardonnay was perfect, slightly sweet yet tart. He chose a truffle to eat and found the nutty taste a perfect complement. "You can trust me."

Her eyes crinkled with laughter. "Where's the fun in that? Kenzie told me you were the instigator."

"Maybe. What about you? You have five brothers and a sister. Where are you in your hierarchy?"

"I'm the third oldest and my two older brothers called me when they needed help getting out of trouble."

"So you were the negotiator." He nodded sagely. Donovan had been the negotiator for him. Not that he could wrap Miss E. around his little finger, but he had a better chance of doing so than Scott or Hunter.

"I guess you could say that. With as many brothers as I had, someone had to negotiate."

"What about your sister?"

"Mara is the baby of the family. She's currently at UC Davis. All she had to do was flutter her eyelashes and she got whatever she wanted, but she shared the bounty. If she got a candy bar, she'd share." A fond smile curved her lips.

Scott wouldn't have shared. Maybe with Kenzie to keep on her good side. "I had a really good time at the car museum today."

Nina sipped her wine and set the glass down. "Me, too. I'm planning a few trips around Reno to some of the other activities tourists can do."

"I'm heading to Virginia City tomorrow." Scott had been planning this one trip since he'd arrived. "When I was a kid I loved anything Western. John Wayne, Roy Rogers, *Bonanza, The Virginian*. I watched the reruns over and over again when I could find them. Virginia City is an old Wild West town that sprang up during the silver and gold rush."

"Are you going to put on a ten-gallon hat, boots and spurs?"

He grinned. He'd been a cowboy for Halloween five years in a row. "I just might, ma'am," he drawled and pretended to tip an invisible hat at her.

"Can I go, too? This I have to see."

His eyebrows rose in surprise. He had to stop himself from yelling out yes. *Play it cool*, he told himself. "Are you inviting yourself along?"

"I think I am."

His heart raced and his hands started to sweat. "I'm really going to just take photos. Photography is my hobby."

"Really. My brother Ben is into photography."

"Then tomorrow's a date." She looked so delectable with the evening breeze tugging at her hair and her face so calm and serene. He couldn't help his next move.

He set his wineglass down, pulled her into his arms and kissed her. Her lips were warm and pleasantly sweet with the wine. Her body leaned into his and he felt every soft curve, smelled her faint perfume, and knew he'd been wanting to kiss her since the moment he'd met her at the bar by the pool.

Chapter 6

Stunned, Nina stood on the balcony. She knew he'd kissed her. The shock of the kiss startled her. Before she could decide what to say, he'd simply left, telling her he'd see her in the morning. She nodded, unable to say anything while her mind processed the kiss.

She liked that kiss. She liked the feel of his hard, muscular body against hers, the sweetness of his breath and the faint scent of his aftershave.

A knock sounded at her door and she almost ran across the suite to fling it open. He'd come back and she waited with breathless anticipation for him to sweep her into his arms and continue on with the kiss and possibly more.

Instead Carl stood in hallway looking nervous. Before she could respond, he leaned toward her to give her an air kiss.

"You've been avoiding me, Nina."

She stepped back before he could pull her into his arms. "Not really." For a brief second, she was almost glad to see Carl. With Carl to distract her, she wouldn't have to think about her and Scott. If she thought about that kiss, she would have to do something and she wasn't certain how to proceed.

"Can I come in?" Carl asked.

She stood aside and gestured him into the suite. He

walked around seeing the open bottle of wine and her glass, which she'd placed there. Scott's glass was still out on the balcony. Carl opened a cabinet and found a wineglass and poured a glass for himself. Nina had to stop herself from telling him no. She didn't want to share that bottle with him.

He sat down just as Kong peeked out of the bedroom and ran out to jump on the sofa and cuddle up next to Carl. Nina found herself smiling. Carl loved animals and Kong adored him as much as the little dog adored her. How could she not like Carl when animals loved him, too? That always told her there was a kindness in him that he seldom showed.

She poured wine into her glass and glanced out at the balcony. Scott's glass was hidden in the shadow and she breathed a sigh of relief because she didn't want to explain anything to Carl.

"You have to help me, Nina." He sipped the wine. "Nice wine. You always did have good taste."

"In some things."

He settled back and studied her, his eyes narrowed. "You look good." He sniffed. "What perfume are you wearing?"

"Nanette."

"It smells good on you."

"Thank you. What's wrong?"

He took a deep breath. Nina sat in a chair and watched him.

"My career is in the toilet," he moaned.

"You work continually. I read in *Variety* that you have three movies coming out next year. How can your career be in the toilet?"

Agitated, he jumped to his feet and started pacing. "Two of those movies are straight to video. Who wants to watch

Shark-A-Conda? *Blood in the Water*? Or…" He ran his hands through his hair as he paced. "*Aliens X*? I've gone from big-budget films to films on a dime. My last film had a budget of $700,000. And most of that went into special effects rather than name actors."

"And it made thirty million in video and you got a nice percentage of that. And from what I'm hearing, it's turning into a cult classic on the Syfy channel." Nina watched him, almost feeling sorry for him. Somewhere on his journey he'd lost sight of the types of films he'd wanted to produce and direct.

"But that's not who I am."

"Stop pacing, you're giving me a headache. Sit down." She pointed at the sofa.

"What happened?" He dropped onto the sofa. "Where did I go wrong?"

"You turned into that obnoxious little director who burned every professional bridge I built for you." Nina's voice came out slightly bitter. She'd believed in him, but he hadn't truly believed in himself.

Kong whimpered and Carl picked the little dog up and hugged him. Kong licked his face. "At least you love me."

"Tiffani loves you, too."

He looked up, tears sparkling in his eyes. "Tiffani left me today. She told me she didn't sign on to follow the ex to Reno."

"Oh, Carl." She reached out to touch him, feeling sorry for him, for the mess he'd made of his career and his life.

"I need you, Nina." He gave her his puppy-dog look. Now if Scott gave her that look, she'd do anything for him. But Carl? Hell, no.

"What do you want?"

"Warner Brothers is developing a project that I'm perfect for."

She thought about that for a second. Was he talking about the new comic book hero being developed to take advantage of the current popularity of superheroes? "You want to direct *Star Chaser*?"

He nodded.

Nina sat back, stunned. "I'm not that good, Carl."

"Yes, you are. At least get me an interview with Jack Reston." He gave her his best pleading look. "He owes you. Your promotional campaign for *Minefield* turned a middling movie into a blockbuster. The critics hated it, even Jack hated it."

"I'll think about it, Carl." She took her dog out of his arms. "You need to go." She pulled him to his feet.

"Please, Nina."

"Just go." He made her feel used.

"Promise you'll think about it."

"I promise." She shoved him toward the door.

He opened the door and instead of air kisses, he kissed her on the lips. "Thank you."

She pushed him out the door, closed it tightly behind him and twisted the dead bolt. He'd kissed her. A half hour ago, Scott had kissed her. She didn't want Carl's kiss to taint her lips.

Scott waited for Nina in the lobby. People streamed through the lobby either checking in or checking out. His camera bag was slung over his shoulder.

"A second date," Hunter said. He handed Scott his coffee. Hunter wore jeans, boots and a plaid shirt open at the throat. He and Lydia must have plans for the day.

"We're visiting Virginia City to take photographs. What are you implying?"

Hunter's dark brown eyes shimmered with mischief. "You went to the car museum yesterday, today you're heading out on another excursion. That's seems kind of intense."

"We're not dating. She's scouting tourist traps and I'm just taking photos."

Hunter chuckled. "Is that what the kids call dating now?"

Scott wanted to punch his brother. "I'm bigger and stronger, bro. Keep this up and you'll be missing a few teeth."

"Just get the teeth you knocked out when I was twelve."

Scott glared at Hunter. Lydia Montgomery entered the lobby with her daughter, Maya, in tow. Saved by the future in-laws. Scott breathed a sigh of relief now he didn't have to talk about the mess that was his love life.

"Hunter," Maya yelled. "Come on, we're going to be late for our riding lessons."

"Got to go, bro," Hunter said. "I have a nondate with a horse and my two best girls." Maya giggled as she tucked her hand in his.

Lydia grinned and tucked her hand around Hunter's elbow. Scott tried not to be jealous. His brother, the first to fall, looked happy. For all her daintiness, Lydia was no pushover.

"Have fun." Scott grinned at Maya.

"We will," Maya said. "Hunter hasn't fallen off for two whole weeks."

Hunter waved as the lobby doors slid open letting in a trace of morning heat.

Scott's grin widened. The elevator door opened and Nina stepped out. She wore jeans and a multi-colored floral T-shirt that suited her. She carried a purse in one hand and a floppy straw hat in the other. She practically bolted across the lobby, sliding to a stop in front of Scott.

"Let's get out of here before Carl finds me…again."

She grabbed his hand and tugged him out the doors into the morning heat. What a take-charge woman! He liked it.

Once in the car, Nina settled in. Scott turned on the air-conditioning and pulled out of the parking lot. In minutes, they were heading south toward Virginia City.

"About last night," Nina said. "I just want you to know I'm totally cool that we had a nice little kiss, but it can't happen again because you're my best friend's brother and it's awkward. I understand why it happened. But it's not going to happen again."

A confusion of thoughts spun through him. "Okay."

Nina frowned at him. "I was expecting more of a fight from you."

That would be laying his cards on the table and he didn't do that. "Are you disappointed?"

"I believe I am." She slumped down in the seat, staring out the window at the city rushing by.

"You're the one who just stated we needed to keep a professional distance between us. I was agreeing. You're blowing one little kiss way out of proportion." The memory of her lips on his heated his blood and despite agreeing with her, he wanted more, a lot more. Why should Nina feel so unnerved by a kiss unless she was feeling something, too?

Something had stirred in Scott, a distant feeling that he'd never felt before. He'd thought he'd been in love before but this feeling was different.

"What's the big deal, Nina?"

"I don't have time for a relationship." Her voice sounded weak as though she wasn't certain she believed herself. "Getting Rio in Reno off the ground is a big task."

"Nina, it was a kiss. We're grown-ups. Kisses happen."

"I'm too busy. This project is the biggest one I've ever done."

"I'm okay with keeping our relationship on a professional level." He tried not to sound disappointed. Or relieved, because Nina was a situation he was sure he could navigate.

"Fine, if that's the way you want to keep things." Did she sound disappointed?

"Stop," Scott commanded in his military command voice. "You're confusing me. If you want to kiss me again that's fine. If you don't, that's fine, too."

"Now you're mad at me."

"Let's put this all aside and have a fun time. Tomorrow will come soon enough."

She sighed.

An uncomfortable silence stretched between them. Scott concentrated on driving, managing the twisty mountain road skillfully.

The town was only a few blocks long with a two-lane street down the center. The street was bordered by original buildings and already tourists walked the plank sidewalks. A roadblock stopped them and a police officer directed them to a side street where Scott found a place to park.

"Where do we start?" Nina asked as she settled her sun hat on her head.

"We'll start on this end and work our way up."

They arrived on the main street to find a group of soldiers in Civil War costumes. Others in period costumes roamed the sidewalks.

"Looks like we're in the middle of the Civil War," Nina said, her gaze darting up and down the street taking in the reenactors. She smiled, her face lighting up. "Get your camera out. This is going to be awesome."

Scott grinned. Excitement coursed through him. He couldn't have planned it better if he'd tried. He loved to watch military reenactments.

"This is great. This is great," Nina muttered as she

wrestled her iPhone out of her purse and started recording notes and taking photos. She switched to her Twitter feed and sent out her first tweet of the day and attached one of the photos.

Scott pulled his Canon out of the camera bag and looped the lanyard around his neck. He fiddled with the adjustments while Nina stared at two women in fancy crinolines as they paused to give directions to a family of tourists. He started snapping photos of the buildings and the people on the street.

"This is exciting," he said.

"You've done the real thing. Where's the excitement in watching adults playact? I'm not trying to be insulting."

"This is living, breathing history." He stopped to snap a photo of a horse-drawn wagon. "We're viewing a piece of the past that has its own romanticism built into it."

"I wouldn't want to live in the past."

"Why not?"

A horrified look passed over her face. "Let's just start with indoor plumbing. I don't have that little apparatus that allows men to tinkle in the woods."

"You don't like to camp, I take it." Not that he was surprised. Nina was a silk-sheet-and-mint-on-the-pillow type. For her he could be, too.

"The last time I camped was at the Waldorf in New York. What is romantic about this?" She spread her hands to indicate the street.

"It's about keeping the past alive, about understanding the past."

"Some parts of our history aren't romantic," she said with a frown.

"What happened happened—we can't change it. We need to remember the past so we don't repeat it in the future."

"Tell that to Congress." Her voice took a sour note.

"Listen, we're just here to have fun today. So let's have fun."

She looked around and suddenly jumped. "Look, a jewelry store." She grabbed his arm and tugged him across the street to the store with the sign The Silver Lode over the window.

When she entered the jewelry store, Scott stayed outside on the boardwalk, watching a line of Union soldiers march down the street. Behind them a horse pulled a cannon. He snapped his photos, taking time to work out how he wanted the position of the soldiers against the backdrop of the buildings. A railroad car doubled as a museum next to an old brick fire station with a bell tower. His camera made clicking noises as he panned the street, humming a little to himself and planning how he would showcase his photos.

Nina studied the rows of glass cases and the brilliantly polished silver chains, pendants, rings and everything a girl could desire.

"This is all so beautiful," she said to the woman behind the counter.

"Thank you. I design my own jewelry." The woman was small and round with her ash-blond hair pulled into a long ponytail hanging down her back. She wore a pioneer-type costume made of light brown fabric. "My name is Beth Greene."

"You could sell this jewelry on Melrose Avenue in Los Angeles. It's just the right kind of funky."

Beth grinned. "I have a contact there and I sell a few pieces a month, but nothing major. Most of my sales are internet and here during tourist season."

Nina's mind raced. Sometimes, she just couldn't keep

the ideas from flowing. "What about any of the casinos in Reno?"

Beth shook her head. "Hotels want touristy stuff and I don't cater to that group."

"Do you mind if I get some photos of some of your pieces?" She pulled a business card out of her purse and handed it to Beth. "I'm working with the Casa de Mariposa in increasing their profile. They're revamping their image and I think you could do some major sales in the gift shop. We're looking for eclectic, one-of-a-kind pieces. I can put you in touch with the buyer."

Beth tilted her head and gave a half smile. "I can see doing a few pieces for a hotel."

"I think I'm going to purchase that one right there. My mother will love it." The silver necklace was shaped like a Mardi Gras mask with a spray of feathers over the mask portion. The chain consisted of delicate loops.

"What about for yourself?" Beth was a salesperson. She opened the back of the case and pulled out a silver cuff bracelet etched with swirls. "This would look nice against your skin." She held the bracelet out to Nina.

Nina slid the cuff over her wrist and knew it was perfect. "I'll take it."

The bell on the door sounded as the door swung open. Scott stepped inside. "Come on, there's going to be a mock battle and I want photos of it."

Nina glanced at Beth and mouthed, *oh yay.* Beth grinned back. "Before we run off after the soldiers, I want some photos of some of her pieces to show Kenzie when she gets back from Brazil."

She gestured at Beth to choose what she wanted photographed. Quickly, Beth unfolded a black velvet cloth and pulled out several pieces. Scott snapped the photos and before Nina could wave goodbye, pulled her out of the store. She went gracefully since she'd been tugging at him since they'd arrived.

The battles lines were already drawn by the time Nina and Scott arrived at the huge field just outside the town. Participants had arranged themselves into position and watchers stood outside the battlefield.

Nina had never seen a mock battle before. Scott paced back and forth down the field taking photos. Nina stood on the sidelines watching. It was more exciting than she thought it would be, though smoke from the huge cannons filled the air and kept her from seeing clearly. But the shouts from the sidelines and the charges where the soldiers clashed in hand-to-hand battle had her jumping up and down, joining in with the audience in shouting encouragement to the two sides. Nina found herself taking a few photos and posting them on Facebook and Twitter.

"Are you enjoying yourself?" Scott asked.

"Very much," she said. Carl loved basketball and she'd gone with him to Lakers and Clippers games. Basketball didn't turn her on, but making connections had. Everyone who was anyone headed to the games, sitting in the courtside seats being photographed, being seen. Carl had season tickets every year. While he'd avidly watched the game, she'd chatted with producers, directors and actors. She never did business, but being social was just as important as making the contacts. Here with Scott she didn't feel the pressure to work; she wanted only to enjoy herself. It was a nice feeling.

The battle ended, and the crowd dispersed back to the main street. Scott headed toward an antique store advertising military memorabilia. While he browsed inside, Nina stayed out on the street.

Usually when Nina planned something fun, it would be going to a museum, gallery openings or parties where she would rub elbows with the movers and shakers of the entertainment industry. A military reenactment had never been on her radar, but seeing it in action gave her a thrill. She'd never thought history could be exciting. History had been nothing but dull facts in a textbook filled with more dull facts. Seeing history in action was a completely different story.

She found a bench to sit on and people-watched. She took a few more photos with her iPhone and attached the best ones to her next tweet. Taking the moment to really look at things, she was surprised at the number of African-American soldiers and suitably costumed women wandering the street. Virginia City was like Comic Con for history buffs—people in costumes, role-paying, having fun by not being themselves.

She had a friend who made documentary films who would love this. Okay, so she didn't leave work too far behind. She took out her phone and texted Stephanie, asking her if she'd ever thought about Civil War reenactments.

"How about some lunch?" Scott said.

"We're not going to re-enact a Civil War lunch, are we?"

"If that's what you want, I can catch you a rabbit."

She stood up and grinned at him. That was just so manly. "Do you know how to catch a rabbit?"

"I can catch anything."

"That's a statement with a lot of meanings."

"You take it however you need to." He grabbed her hand and led her toward a building advertising lunch specials. At least she wouldn't be cooking over a fire. "And after lunch, we need to visit the cemeteries."

She stopped and he kept walking a few steps before realizing she wasn't with him. "What's so fascinating about a cemetery? Are there beautiful headstones? Marble angels? What?"

"There's a lot of history in cemeteries." He opened the door to the restaurant and led her inside.

A hostess, dressed in a prairie-style gown and boots, took them to a table overlooking the street. Her footsteps echoed off the plank floor. The interior of the restaurant was quaint and diverse. The wood tables with wooden chairs were all different styles and colors. The only unifying elements were the red-and-white checked plastic tablecloths and the cowboy and cowgirl costumes on the waitstaff. Old photos of Virginia City decorated the walls. Lights designed to look like oil lamps hung over every table. Almost all the tables were filled with families.

This was the oddest date she'd ever been on, but she was enjoying herself beyond all expectations.

"Next week they're having camel races." He opened a brochure and showed her a photo of a camel.

"No way," Nina said. "I didn't know camels could be raced." Another thing to add to her events log. "Do you want to go?"

"I was thinking more along the lines of telling Hunter so he can bring Lydia and Maya. Maya would love the camel races. I should bring her."

"I don't know about that," Nina said. "She'd want a camel." Nina had only met Maya a few days ago and already she was pestering her mother for a dog like Kong.

"I know, and I want to watch my brother deal with the situation." He chuckled as he folded the brochure and tucked it into a side pocket on his camera bag.

Who knew he had such a devilish sense of humor. Why this gorgeous, sexy and fun man was running around free range was beyond her. "That's evil."

"I know."

"I thought you were supposed to be the serious one."

"There's a side to me no one knows about." He chuckled

again and rubbed his hands together. "Evil is fun. Payback is a younger brother's prerogative."

"Remind me to never get on your bad side." Or maybe that would be even more fun.

"With all the work you're going to cause, you may have a permanent spot on my bad side."

"Don't you want the hotel to be a success?"

"I do, actually. But at the moment, we're not prepared to be a success."

A waitress approached for their order. Nina ordered a BLT and Scott ordered a hamburger with fries.

"What do you need to do to make the hotel and casino safe for its guests?"

"Probably fire sixty percent of the security staff who think the hotel is their personal ATM."

"What do you intend to do?"

"I had a little get-to-know-you meeting with the union reps and basically I have to have permission from God to fire anyone." He rubbed the bridge of his nose.

The meeting had obviously not gone well. "How are you going to get rid of the bad apples?"

"I have my ways."

"Do tell."

The waitress brought their drinks. Nina unwrapped the paper napkin from around her knife and fork. She took a sip of her iced tea and sighed. She hadn't known how thirsty she was. She drank half the glass before she realized it. The waitress grinned at her and headed back to the table with a full pitcher to replenish her tea.

Again, a grin spread across his face. "My job is to keep the hotel and casino safe, and to do that I'm having my people get caught up on their firearms certification, physical requirements and psychological evaluations. I could have a lot of fun with this."

Nina stared at him in awe. This guy could work in Hollywood. "You are evil."

"The security force is responsible for the safety and well-being of our guests. They need a lot of training."

"Are you treating them like they're in the military?"

"I'm weeding my garden."

The food came. They paused in their conversation while the waitress set their food in front of them. Nina smiled at her sandwich and the pile of bacon in it.

"What about the good ones? Aren't you afraid you'll lose them?"

"They'll do what they have to do to keep their jobs. The bad ones are looking for an easy payoff."

"If I want to get rid of someone I just put out some bad press. Seems to me you're doing a lot of work." Nina took a bite of her sandwich and breathed deeply in satisfaction. This was the best BLT she'd had in a long time.

"Got to be done." Scott bit into his hamburger and looked up in surprised satisfaction. Then he said, "What is amazing to me is what a casino can be held responsible for. People think that some places are the spot to let their hair down and sow some wild oats. Then they do something stupid and want to blame the hotel. Or they complain about everything and nothing at the same time."

Nina enjoyed watching him eat. He savored every bite the way her father did. "Your job sounds way harder than mine. People want to work with me and I never worry about them being unqualified." A lot of her business was word of mouth.

Scott's phone rang. He lifted it to his ear and listened for a moment. "Did you call the Secret Service, yet?" Scott paused then spoke again. "Get on that. They have a field office in Reno." He listened again. "Nina and I will be back in about forty-five minutes." He disconnected. "We have to go." He raised a hand for the waitress to pay the bill and as soon as he finished signing his name, he was on his feet.

Nina gulped the last of her iced tea, wrapped the remaining part of her sandwich in a napkin to finish in the car.

"What's going on?" Nina trotted to keep up with him.

"Someone tried to buy a $3,000 necklace with counterfeit bills." He darted down a side street and speed walked to the car. Nina jogged to keep up with his long-legged stride.

"That sounds ominous."

"If not for a sharp-eyed clerk, he might have gotten away with it." The car chirped when he unlocked it.

Nina jumped inside and was buckled up as he backed out of the parking spot. The SUV jumped forward when he hit the accelerator too hard. Getting out of town was slow with so many pedestrians darting across the streets. Finally he left Virginia City behind for the twisting mountain road that would take them back to the highway and Reno.

"Don't you ever get a day off?" Nina had enjoyed being with him, being in the quaint little town that owed its roots to the Comstock Lode.

"I'll get a day off when the security issues at the casino and the hotel are solved."

"Will they be solved?"

"They will when I have all the right people in place."

"Do casinos have a problem with counterfeit bills? I should think people would know right away when they see one." Nina watched the countryside roll away and felt a tiny tingle of apprehension at the thought.

"It's a great place to launder money. Even nowadays with all the cash cards and digital printouts and cameras, a segment of people still pay cash for everything. A big winner who wins thirteen or fourteen thousand dollars will go shopping with their winnings. Last night I watched some guy pay cash for a watch that cost seventeen thousand dollars. He went from the blackjack table to the jewelry store."

"How come you watched him buy a watch?"

"I was making sure he got to his destination with all the cash. He even tipped the salesgirl."

"So basically that's the kind of customer a casino wants," Nina mused. "Someone who wins in the casino and spends his winnings in the jewelry store."

"Circle of life, Reno style," Scott said.

"That's what I want to do. Keep those people in the casino by giving them a good time." And providing them with the luxury items they'd likely purchase with their winnings.

"A lot of money goes through a casino," Scott continued. "A certain percentage is going to be counterfeit."

"How does someone know?"

"We have marking pens, machines that can spot it, but the first line of defense is the people who handle the cash. They can tell a counterfeit bill by the feel, the look and just plain instinct. Miss E. told me that she knew someone who could smell bad money."

"I should think that with today's digital cameras, which can photograph the finest details, it would be easy to make your own money."

"Cameras can capture all the correct detail on a bill, but printers don't have the same output. The U.S. Treasury uses a specific kind of paper with a specific kind of ink."

"So it's easy in the early stages, but more difficult in the output."

"Exactly."

Nina fell silent as she mused about the fake money. She realized it wasn't her problem, but in a way it was. The people she wanted to attract to the casino needed to know they were safe. Maybe Scott had a bigger problem on his hands than he knew.

Chapter 7

Scott entered the interview room. Belle Sampson sat across from a man with sandy-blond hair, faded blue eyes and a fair complexion. He was about as nondescript as a person could be, dressed in khaki pants and a plain, white knit shirt. He practically blended into the beige wall behind him.

"Belle," Scott said.

"Hi, boss." She jumped to her feet and smiled at him. "Meet George Williams. George this is Scott Russell. He heads security here at the Casa de Mariposa."

"George, you seem to be in a bit of trouble." Scott leaned against the table, towering over the man.

George looked up, but his gaze immediately slid away as he looked back down at his hands. "I didn't do nothing wrong. I got to be gettin' home. My wife is gonna worry." His voice was a whiny mumble that Scott strained to hear.

"Tell me your side of the story."

"I won three grand at the blackjack table over at the Ruby Slipper. I wanted to buy my wife something pretty. So I went to Diamonte's." He clenched his hands and refused to look up. "I didn't know the bills was fake."

"I see. I tell you what. I'm going to check on your story and I'll be back in a bit. Are you hungry? I can have a sandwich or something sent up from the kitchen."

George glanced up. "That would be nice. Thank you."

"Coffee, soda, tea?"

"Coffee would be good." George looked back down at his hands.

Scott patted him on the shoulder and smiled at Belle. Her own smile was almost predatory as she reached for the phone to call the kitchen. "The store manager is in your office with Gary."

Scott nodded and made his way across the hall to his office.

Gary White sat in Scott's chair, his feet on the desk, trying to look like he was in charge. With one look from Scott, Gary immediately put his feet on the floor and sat up straight. Scott continued to look at him until he realized he was sitting in Scott's chair. Gary jumped to his feet, his face going red. A touch of anger showed in his eyes and Scott wondered why.

"This is Amanda Freeman. She's the manager at the Diamonte," Gary said, his tone a little sullen. He gestured at the woman who stood at Scott's entrance.

Amanda Freeman was slim and elegant looking in a dove-gray suit that set off her café au lait skin to perfection. Wavy black hair was slicked back into a tidy bun at the back of her head.

"Thank you for waiting for me," Scott said. He sat on the corner of his desk. "Tell me what happened."

"He's been in the Diamonte before with the same story he gave me last time."

"And what was that?" Scott coaxed.

"Crystal waited on him last time. He told her he'd won three grand at the blackjack table at the Ruby Slipper, wanted to buy something pretty for his wife and he liked the jewelry we carried. I didn't pay much attention at the time because I hear that story a couple times a day. But when I cashed out that night, I discovered I had nearly twenty-seven counterfeit bills in hundreds. And he was the only one who made a big purchase that day." Amanda frowned. "And today when he walked in, I recognized him right away. He gave me the same story, picked out a necklace for his wife and forked over the money. The top three bills were genuine, but the rest of the money was counterfeit. I told him I would have to confiscate the counterfeit bills and he started to get belligerent with me. I called security and Belle arrived within two minutes."

Scott nodded as she talked. "Thank you for your help. You can head back to work."

"I'm closing tonight so I'll be here until around nine-thirty."

"Good. You'll have to tell your story to the Secret Service when they get here. I'll give you a buzz when they're ready for you." Scott opened the door to his office and allowed Amanda to leave. He turned to Gary White. "You did call them?"

Gary nodded. "I talked to an agent, Pierce Calderon, who said he'd be here within the hour, but he hasn't arrived yet."

"Thanks for taking care of that. Go on back to work and if I need you I'll let you know."

Gary opened the door at the same moment a tall, lean man knocked. He wore a plain dark blue suit and carried a hat in one hand. The slightest hint of a bulge at the side under his arm told Scott he was armed.

"I'm looking for Scott Russell," the man said. "I'm Pierce Calderon, U.S. Secret Service. I hear you got yourself someone passing counterfeit money." He handed his badge and ID to Scott who studied it carefully.

Scott held out his hand. "I'm Russell. I've got a guy named George Williams who says he won three thousand at blackjack at the Ruby Slipper and just wanted to buy something nice for his wife. But the store manager saw that most of the money was counterfeit."

"Good ole George, though last month he was Harry, and Bertram the month before that." Pierce said, shaking Scott's hand. "We've been after him for a while. He's been traveling all over Nevada and California passing funny money and buying jewelry, which he resells on eBay. Makes a tidy little profit. We put out an alert to all the casinos."

"I'm still playing catch-up. I'll look for the alert and make sure it's posted in the retail areas. George-Harry-Bertram is all yours."

"Thanks for getting him."

Scott led the way across the hall. He paused before opening the door to the interview room. "How about helping me with a training program to educate the vendors? If not for the sharp eyes of the store manager, George would have gotten away with passing the fake bills a second time."

"I hear you're new in town and have some security issues here. I'll be happy to help you set up a training program."

"Thanks," Scott replied. He opened the door to the interview room and allowed Pierce to precede him. George looked up, shifting uneasily in his chair. Scott and Pierce sat across from him. Scott nodded at Belle who immediately stood up and went to stand by the door.

"Hello, George," Pierce said, his smile sharklike. "I've been looking for you."

Nina sat on the floor, knitting needles clicking. She'd taken a break from her planning and wanted to finish the booties she was currently knitting for Jack Reston's new baby boy.

Her laptop sat on the coffee table and papers were spread out as she studied the outline of her promotional campaign. At the moment, it looked like everything was chaos, but Nina's experienced eye saw the way things were coming together. Eydie had started on the website and sent a preliminary report to Nina. Nina liked what she saw, but made notes on some changes she wanted. She planned to commission Scott to take more photos of the hotel and the casino to be posted on the website.

She tried to concentrate on her knitting, but her mind kept going back to Scott and their trip to Virginia City. She'd had a good time and wanted to plan another outing with him. Scott may have been deadly serious, but he had a fun streak. She wanted to see more of the funnier, laid-back side of him.

A knock sounded at the door. Kong lifted his head from where he'd been asleep on the sofa and gave a tentative bark.

"Some watchdog you are." Nina scratched him behind the ears affectionately.

She pushed herself up and found Anastasia Parrish standing in the doorway, her tiny dog, Duchess, tucked firmly in her purse with just her head poking out.

"Hi, I know I'm a little early for Duchess and Kong's playdate."

Three days early to be precise. She stood aside for Anastasia to enter. "I was just about to have a snack. Can I interest you in some cheese and crackers? I found this lovely Brie at the market down the street. And these delightful little crackers. Iced tea or coffee?"

"Sounds wonderful. Coffee, please." Anastasia set her purse on a table and lifted Duchess out. Duchess jumped at Kong, who eyed her as though he were being pestered by a fly.

Anastasia followed Nina into the small kitchenette. Anastasia looked around. "How homey."

Nina shrugged. She'd seen the huge penthouse suite Anastasia had claimed for her own. "Compared to your suite, it's pretty small."

"I was so surprised at how luxurious the penthouse suite was. This hotel constantly surprises me."

"Wealthy women from all over the United States used to come here for a quickie divorce."

"I thought that was Las Vegas."

"Las Vegas," Nina said, "was the marriage capital of the U.S., Reno was the divorce capital."

Anastasia looked confused. "Did you come here for your divorce?"

"No."

"I hear you didn't get much from the divorce settlement."

Nina's eyebrows rose. "I got the most important things. My dog, my shoes and my pride."

"When I get a divorce…" Anastasia said.

"Did you get married?" Nina asked, confused. She'd always had a hard time following Anastasia's logic.

"No. Not yet. I'm planning ahead."

"Maybe that was my problem." Nina opened the Brie and set it on a plate. She popped the plate into the microwave for a few seconds until the cheese softened just enough to spread. She started the coffeemaker and poured iced tea into her own glass.

"In my social stratosphere…" Anastasia spread her hands over her chest. "We have to plan ahead."

Nina was surprised Anastasia even knew the word stratosphere. *Be nice*, Nina chided herself. Underneath the arrogance and superiority, Anastasia was a predictably nice person. "Planning ahead has merits, but it does smack of taking all the romance out of a marriage."

Anastasia shrugged. "You mean you married Carl for love. You're so brave."

Irritated at the thought that Anastasia made her sound like a fireman or a policeman charging into a burning building to save a baby, Nina tore open the plastic encasing the crackers and a few burst into crumbs. She set the crackers on the plate and added a jar of strawberry preserves. She loved a hint of strawberry on top of the Brie. She set the plate on the counter. Anastasia hopped on a bar stool and attacked the Brie.

"You got out in time." Anastasia's voice dropped to an intimate whisper. "I hear his career is in the toilet."

"Why are you whispering?" Nina asked.

"I don't want anyone to overhear us. Just in case your room is bugged."

"Really," Nina said. "I don't think you need to worry about it here."

"You've no idea how many times Daddy and I arrived at some hotel to find a dozen bugs in every room."

"I'm pretty sure you're safe here."

Anastasia bit into a cracker and smiled. "This is heavenly. And I can't take any chances. Daddy handles classified material all the time. You never know who's listening."

The dogs had finally gotten over their shyness and started running back and forth, play-growling. Duchess had one of Kong's squeaky toys and teased him before running away.

Anastasia took another bite of cracker and grinned at Nina. "How was your date with Scott last Sunday? I saw some of your tweets. One of them mentioned a jewelry store. I must have the name. I loved your photos and I think I'll take a quick trip down."

Nina was surprised. "You read my tweets! I'm so surprised you follow me on Twitter."

"Nina, your Twitter and Facebook accounts are the most interesting around. You have almost as many followers as some of the A-list celebrities and of course, me."

The queen of the back-handed insult had spoken. "Thank you." *I think.* Nina used her tweets to promote her accounts. She'd only just started working out her Twitter campaign on what she wanted to say about the hotel.

"I loved when you outfitted Kong at the doggy boutique in New York. He's their unofficial mascot."

"He did look cute in his pirate costume," Nina admitted. Kong was photogenic and he knew how to pose the minute the camera came out.

"You didn't answer my question," Anastasia pouted.

No she hadn't. In fact, her relationship with Scott was none of Anastasia's business, but Nina was too diplomatic to say so out loud. "Virginia City is very interesting. They were having a Civil War reenactment and scores of men were dressed as soldiers and the women wore period gowns. Scott took lots of photos."

Anastasia nodded. "He's an amazing amateur photographer. You should get him a show in a gallery. His photos are museum-quality good. I tried to get something set up for him back in DC, but he wouldn't cooperate." Her mouth turned down as though Scott's decision had been a personal affront to her.

Nina understood why Scott wouldn't allow her to help him. Anastasia was the last woman in the world a person wanted to owe a favor to. In fact, Anastasia owed Nina a favor for making her look good at the disaster of T-Rex's party. Nina doubted she'd say anything. Anastasia preferred to have people in her debt and not the other way around.

They finished the Brie and crackers. Nina poured more coffee into Anastasia's cup.

"What's really on your mind, Anastasia?" Nina finally asked. The woman hadn't come for a playdate. She wanted something from Nina. "What can I do for you?"

"I like Scott."

Who doesn't, Nina thought, waiting for Anastasia to get her thoughts together. "Go on."

"I want to find out if you're interested in him, or if the path is clear for me." Anastasia sipped her coffee, her eyes narrowed as she watched Nina for a reaction.

If Scott was the least bit interested in Anastasia, he would never have left Washington, DC. He'd had years to establish his interest and the fact that he hadn't was telling.

"Well," Nina said, "if you're interested, have at it." Because that was going to be a hell of a show watching her fail.

"Daddy is desperate for Scott to come to work for him. He's the best in the security business and Daddy always wants the best."

"Is that why you came to Reno? You're trying to lure him into service to your father."

"Of course."

From the look in Anastasia's eyes, she herself had more than a passing interest. But then again, Anastasia made a habit of dating men her daddy didn't approve of. She had a special fondness for musicians and actors. Daddy wanted her to make a diplomatic marriage and she wanted to be wild and in the spotlight. Her father wanted Scott to work for him just to keep Anastasia out of trouble. No wonder Scott had left DC. This woman was one step away from being a stalker.

Nina leaned forward on her elbows. "So you want Scott." Now her hackles were up, but she wasn't going to let anyone see that.

Anastasia nodded as though she'd already won.

"Then," Nina continued, "you need to win over his family. Family is very important to Scott. And I suggest you start with Miss E., his grandmother."

Anastasia giggled. "Oh, sweet little old ladies love me."

Nina tried to keep the satisfaction out of her voice. "Then make yourself indispensable to Miss E. Get on her good side."

Anastasia slid off the stool. "Thank you for your wonderful advice. I've had a good time. Talk to you later." She scooped Duchess off the floor and tucked the wriggling dog back into her purse. "Bye." She waved, opened the door and left before Nina could say anything else.

"Have fun." Nina waved at the closed door, trying not to laugh. Miss E. was going to eat that woman for breakfast. Should she feel a little guilty? Not a chance.

Scott spent the afternoon printing out some of the photos he'd taken at Virginia City. He spread them out on the dining room table liking what he saw.

He'd managed to capture Nina in several of them looking casual and relaxed with the wind blowing her hair back. She was incredibly beautiful and all that bundled energy made him want to be near her all the time. In most of the photos she was talking to someone, a woman in a period gown, a soldier with his musket, a little girl in prairie dress and bonnet. One thing he noticed about her, when she spoke to someone she gave that person every moment of her attention, making them feel they were the most important person in the world at that moment. She made them feel comfortable.

People gravitated to her like she was the sun and they were planets orbiting her. He wasn't a poetic man, but something about her brought out the poetry. Usually he dated serious women. Until Nina, he'd liked serious women.

He picked up the photos of Nina. The few he'd captured of her by herself he'd keep to himself. For some reason he didn't want anyone to see them.

He gathered up the photos he wanted to share with her and placed them in a folder. He reached for the phone and dialed her suite.

"Want to come up to my place for dinner later?" Scott asked when she answered the phone. "I want to show you the photos I took last Sunday."

"That sounds like fun. What time?"

He glanced at his watch. "How about six thirty?"

"I'll be there."

Grinning, Scott disconnected and opened the browser on his laptop to look for Brazilian recipes. His skills weren't as impressive as his brother's, but he could wield a spatula with the best of them. And he so wanted to impress her.

He liked how he felt when he was with her. He wanted to be with her all the time.

He browsed through recipes and printed off a few with names he couldn't pronounce. The food preparation looked simple enough. Now all he had to do was find the food he needed and he was on his way to cooking a meal Nina would never forget.

After an hour on the internet, Scott realized he wasn't going to cook something memorable. He wasn't even certain where to find the spices. He didn't know what *linguiça* was or where he could purchase it. He did find a meat-filled pancake that looked easy enough, *panqueqa de carne.* He didn't have the ingredients on hand, but the hotel kitchen was well-stocked. He printed off the ingredients list and instructions. He could do this. He'd survived the Middle East. He could cook a dinner and impress a girl.

The kitchen was a bustle of activity. Manny Torres stood in the center of the maelstrom issuing orders and showing the newest cooks their jobs. Scott approached the man who wielded a spatula like a conductor.

The kitchen was immaculate. The chaos looked orderly in its own way and the smells of food were heavenly.

"What brings you here?" Manny asked in his slightly accented voice. He may have left Brazil behind in his youth, but the rhythm of the language could still be heard in his voice.

Scott wasn't quite certain what to say. How did he tell this man he wanted to cook for his daughter? Instead he held out the printed pages hoping that would explain what he wanted. "I need the ingredients."

Manny looked them over and gave Scott a shrewd look. "Do you need help making this?" Manny handed the list of ingredients to a passing chef and told him to gather them and put them at Manny's station.

"I think I can manage it."

"Why are you interested in making Brazilian food?"

I want your daughter. He didn't say that but it was up in his thought bubble. "I thought I'd try something different. I thought I'd expand my cultural horizons." Scott tried not to stutter. He might have been a soldier with a lot of battle experience, but something about Manny almost intimidated Scott. This man was the father of a woman Scott was interested in and wanted to impress in some way. He didn't want to share the details. He managed to keep himself from babbling

"I'm glad you didn't choose something with *cuy* in it."

"What is that?"

"You Americans call them guinea pigs. In Peru, they are *cuy* and considered a delicacy."

Kenzie had a guinea pig when she'd been a kid. As much as Scott disliked the noisy thing, he would never have thought to eat it. "No *cuy*."

"Good, my daughter doesn't believe in eating her pets."

Busted. "Excuse me." How did he know Scott was cooking for Nina?

Manny patted him on the shoulder. Even though he was a head shorter than Scott, his presence dominated a room and his energy pushed at the walls.

"Come along. I will help you." Manny grabbed a white coat off from a hook on the wall and pushed it at Scott. "I will make you a cook to please my daughter."

Scott almost shivered. Did Manny know that Scott wanted to do more to his daughter than just cook for her? He wanted to kiss her and maybe not stop at a kiss.

With the dishes completed and warming in the oven, Scott had just enough time to grab a shower and get dressed. By the time he was pulling his shirt over his head, Nina was knocking at the door. He opened the door and stood in front of her in bare feet and his hair still wet.

She looked divine in a peacock-blue-and-green dress that hugged her figure like a second skin. She wore matching green stilettos. She grinned and handed him a bottle of Cabernet. "My dad said to bring red wine. How would he know that?"

Scott chuckled. "I needed some help with dinner."

"You mean you and my dad cooked dinner."

He nodded. "I have to give him his props."

"I'm impressed. What did you make?" She sniffed the air.

"I'll have to show you. I don't think I can pronounce

it." He led her into the kitchen for a peek at the oven and she grinned at him.

"*Panqueqa de carne.* One of my favorites." She grinned at him.

"I thought I'd try something new." He took the bottle of wine and opened it to let it breathe. Yeah, that sounded good but not desperate.

He picked up a file folder and handed it to her. "Take a look."

Nina gasped in delight as she worked her way through the pile of photos. "These are really good."

While she was looking at them, he'd put on shoes and dried his hair. He poured her a glass of wine and set it in front of her.

"You have a good eye." She spread the photos out on the coffee table. "I didn't think I'd be interested in a historical reenactment, but you made it interesting." She didn't get the appeal of reenactments, but the photos changed something in her mind. No modern elements interacted in the photos. Each picture captured people as though they were truly a moment in history. She didn't see one cell phone or car in the background. He'd taken her back in time and she found she could appreciate what she saw.

"Have you ever considered doing a gallery show?" she asked curiously. These photos were definitely of that quality.

"Not really." He looked a little uncomfortable.

"When you were in Afghanistan, did you take photos?"

"Thousands."

"That would be a fascinating exhibit of soldiers' lives from a soldier's point of view." She started thinking about a showing for Veterans Day. That was only about eight weeks off. She could put something together for it. The lobby had a lot of wall space where photos would look perfect.

Scott looked thoughtful as he set the table. "I don't know." He made smooth, precise movements as he put two plates down and arranged silverware around them.

She jumped up and held up the photo for Scott to see. "Look at this photo of this young black man in a Union uniform. He looks real. He's sweating, he's dirty and looks like he's there to fight a war. You caught something intense and genuine. This man is defending his home, he's fighting for his beliefs. You have a raw, powerful talent."

"What do you know about photography?"

"I've worked with enough artists, musicians, filmmakers, stylists and I know what goes into making an album cover, a film poster. A lot goes into the design with the intent to spark an emotional reaction. You've captured those raw emotions so easily." Admiration filled her. For all his attempts to be serious, to be the rock people depended on, Scott Russell had the heart and soul of an artist.

"I'm not going to be one of your projects. I have a job to do. A serious job."

She cocked an eyebrow. "Art is serious. Why did you take the photographs if you think art is nothing but a frivolous pastime?"

"In most of the photos I've taken, I wanted to remember the moment." He opened the oven and took out the food, placing it on the table. He poured more wine into their glasses and held out a chair for Nina. "I never intended to do anything with them."

"Those photos you took in the Middle East. How many of those men and women are gone?"

His face stilled and his eyes showed sadness. "A few."

"What a great way to honor them. I have absolutely

no idea what the day-to-day life of a soldier is like. Most people don't know. I think they should. You weren't taking photos to relax, you were capturing important moments. Moments that need to be shared." She sat down at the table, still clutching the photo of the Union soldier in her hand. She set it down out of the way, but couldn't stop looking at it. She felt that man's pain even though he was only pretending. To that young soldier, the moment was real. "You need to think about doing a showing. Anastasia's mother is a very big patron of the arts. I'm sure with one glance at your photos, she'll get you into any major museum in this country."

"I'll think about it. Let's eat." Scott served the food. "Enjoy."

She grinned at him, delighted in having another project. "Think fast. Veterans Day is right around the corner and we'd only have about six weeks to get this in place."

"I said I'd think about it."

At her first bite, she was lost. The food was delicious and even though he'd made the food himself, she could sense her father's guiding hand. She was totally enchanted. She'd never had a man who'd romanced her with food before. Usually it was the other way around.

After Nina helped him clear the table and put the dishes in the dishwasher, she sat down on the sofa with his photos spread out on the coffee table. She couldn't stop looking at them. Scott had captured some intangible feeling in each one. A mother's look at her adorable daughter perched on her daddy's shoulders. A young soldier gazing happily at the lovely young woman on his arm, her dress billowing to expose the crinoline underneath along with a peak at her ruffled drawers. Nina loved each one.

Scott sat next to her. He offered her a glass of wine and she sipped it and set the glass on the coffee table.

"These photos are just amazing. I can't stop looking at them."

"Thank you," he replied. He slid an arm around her and pulled her close.

She nestled against him, loving the warmth of his body, the firmness of his muscles and the faint hint of spiciness that clung to him. She inhaled deeply, her eyes closed.

He ran a hand down her arm and her skin tingled.

"I..." she said.

"Shush." He ran his finger over her mouth and then kissed her.

Nina leaned into the kiss. His lips were velvety smooth. His breath was sweet and fresh. Warmth flooded through her, settling at her core. She moaned and pushed closer. Closer.

Every nerve ending came alive. Her breasts grew tight and her nipples hardened. Deep down inside a flame grew and she gasped when he gently ran his thumb over a nipple. His touch was so light, she pushed into it. His lips were soft as they nibbled at her ear, her cheek and the corner of her mouth.

Each breath he took fanned her cheek. Every touch of his fingers sent tingles of heat vibrating through her.

Somehow they'd ended up in the bedroom wearing barely any clothes.

His kisses grew deeper as they lay on the bed. His hands roamed her body so lightly she moaned. He was bold, then tender, and confident. His finger edged around her nipple and down her stomach to hesitate at the band of her silk panties. She was wet and pliant and she grabbed his hand and pushed it where she wanted it. A finger gently teased her nub before easing down farther and sliding inside her.

* * *

A hungry glint shone in Nina's brown eyes. She arched up; soft moans sounded. He liked kissing her. She was so tender and passionate. He didn't want the kiss to end.

Her hands moved up his body, leaving a trail of heat. She trembled in his arms, her heart racing.

Slowly he pushed the dark curtain of her hair aside. His fingers caressed the sensitive skin on her neck and slowly moved down to a taut nipple. Her skin was flawless, smooth as silk, broken only by the tiny pink triangle of silk that covered her core. She was sublime, she was perfect.

Scott trailed kisses down her stomach to the silk triangle. He hooked his thumbs over the strings keeping it in place. Sighing, she raised her hips and he gently pulled the triangle away from her body and down her long smooth legs.

He sat back and smiled at the sight of her open and exposed to him. He ran his hands up her supple body, stopping at the juncture of her thighs to ease his fingers inside her again.

She cried out and he gently kissed her nub. She smelled like sin. She was the nectar of the gods.

He planted a kiss on her stomach. Her whole body trembled.

She started to take off her shoes, but he stopped her. The sight of a woman who wore nothing but a pair of decadent high heels did things to a man's head and another area on his body. Goose bumps rose on her skin and he could smell desire, feel her heat. If he didn't get inside her soon he was going to die.

Slowly he worked his mouth up her body, the quivering stomach, and her silky skin, back to her breasts. He stood and put his hands on her wrist and stared into her brown eyes. "I need you."

Nina nodded and her body relaxed. Her eyes clouded over with the depth of her passion and need.

Her breasts were round, high and firm, perfection of the highest order. The dusky nipples, hardened to chocolate peaks, were an invitation to suckle. He took first one nipple and then the other, sucking gently until her stomach clenched and she moaned.

Nina's breath shuddered as he tugged harder on her nipples. She dug her nails into his shoulders. He nipped each tip and she giggled. "Don't you want me to take off my shoes?"

"Hell, no." He ran a hand down the long, slender calf of one leg.

Nina giggled again. "I've never left my shoes on before."

He smiled. "There's always a first."

She bit her bottom lip. He lay next to her and took her hand and guided it to his hardness. She stroked his penis, teasing the tip. He sucked in a deep breath and suddenly grinned at the teasing look at her face.

"Enjoying yourself?" he asked.

"Oh, yes."

He reached into the nightstand for a condom, tore it open and put it on. He couldn't wait any longer to bury himself inside her.

Slowly he spread her legs and eased himself between them. The wetness on her inner lips told him she was more than ready. Gently he eased inside her feeling her tightness. He was lost in her softness.

He kissed her until she was as breathless as he. "You are so beautiful."

She touched his lips with her fingertips. "You make me feel beautiful."

He sucked first one finger and then a second into his

mouth, his tongue twirling around each once. He kneaded her hard nipples, tweaking each one until she gasped.

She tasted so sweet. Her skin was so soft, he could barely contain himself.

"Scott!" she cried.

The way she said his name turned him on even more.

She clutched at him, her hands grabbing his bottom and pulling him down hard inside her. He licked and suckled until he felt her inner muscles clench tightly. She was just seconds from the edge. She thrust harder against him, her hips grinding against his, her core hot and demanding. Her eyes filled with such passion, tears leaked from the sides.

Her inner muscles contracted, clenching and unclenching, creating just the right amount of friction to force his own orgasm. He felt suspended between life and death.

A low moan escaped her lips. She clutched his shoulders. Her orgasm surrounded his penis.

The French called an orgasm *le petit mort*—the little death. And for the first time in his life, he understood why.

"You are incredible," she murmured when her body relaxed.

"You're welcome." He kissed her long and hard. "We are so not done."

"Thank God for that." She kissed him, her tongue twirling around his.

He grew hard again. Her legs gripped his waist. He felt her next orgasm, the muscles tightening, the friction building again.

He couldn't get enough of her. He kissed her lush mouth, her breasts, her neck, he wanted to taste every inch of her. He wanted to mark her, to make her his.

His thrusts increased in speed and force. His heart raced as her heat engulfed him. "Sweet."

"Kiss me."

"Yes," he whispered then took her mouth.

He thrust harder and deeper, carrying her higher. Again, her muscles contracted around him, her back arched and he heard her say his name over and over again, and he let go, spilling himself inside her a second time.

Her arms wrapped around him. "Scott." Her lips trembled and her eyes were passion-glazed.

"Thank you," he said.

She gently touched her mouth to his, her kiss as tender as it had been fierce before. He wanted more of her. He wanted more than her body. He wanted her soul.

Chapter 8

Carl slipped into the booth across from Nina. Nina, fork poised over her cheese omelet, waited. She wasn't certain she wanted Carl disturbing her so early in the morning. She wanted to think about Scott and what had happened between them. Being in his bed had felt so right to her, and she was almost afraid because their lovemaking had been so perfect. Her head still whirled with the depth of her emotions, the complexity of her passion.

Everything about Scott made her whole body tingle with excitement and passion. Their evening had been almost magical. With Carl sitting in front of her, she found herself comparing the two men and realized she shouldn't do that now.

But did she want to get involved with Scott? She'd changed her life, compromised on so many levels for Carl because she had believed in his vision. She wasn't going to do that again. Carl had always been a bit intimidated by her, even as he accepted her for who she was and not for whom he wanted her to be.

Looking back on her marriage to Carl, she always felt that he had an agenda and she was just an item on his to-do list. Everything revolved around him. He was okay with her job, as long as everything came back to him. She'd never noticed this during their marriage, only later when she had time to dissect what had gone wrong.

"Well," Carl said.

"Well, what?"

"Have you talked to Jack Reston, yet?"

"No. I haven't."

A look of disappointment spread over his face. "But…"

"Now is not the time to bother him. His wife just had a baby and you need to find a nice gift to send to them. The baby's name is Milo."

"What should I get a baby?"

"My advice is something personal, but not *I'm stalking you* personal."

"Just tell me what I should buy." Carl looked irritated.

"Check out Tiffany's website. That should give you some ideas."

Carl whipped out his iPhone and started looking.

Nina went back to her breakfast. The waitress brought her another pot of hot water for tea and Nina smiled her thanks. Carl scrolled busily through whatever he'd found.

"Do you think a $28,000 sterling-silver-and-sapphire box is too much?"

"Tone it down, Carl. That's a desperation gift."

He stared at her in surprise. "You're thinking about babies. I'd make a great father."

She shook her head firmly. "No."

"But, Nina…"

"No," she repeated. "I don't want to be married to you anymore, much less have a baby with you."

"But I'd be a great…"

"No, you wouldn't. Do you know why we never had children? Because you wouldn't be the baby anymore. Carl, you're a full-time job."

He looked offended. "Nina, that isn't fair."

"I'm not saying it's fair, but it is true."

He glanced back at his phone. "How about a hand-painted Limoges china alphabet box. Only $215."

"That will work," Nina said. "You can have the baby's name and birthdate painted on the bottom."

"That's it?"

"First of all, they haven't announced the baby's name yet and probably won't for several weeks. The fact that you're having the name painted on means you're on the inside."

"How did you find out the baby's name?"

"Sandra Canfield is going to be the godmother. We talked. So keep it under your hat until the official announcement. She knew I'd be making booties, so she gave me the details."

Carl scrolled across his phone, tapped at it for several minutes, took out a credit card and added that to the order. When he was done he looked up and smiled. "Done." He grinned and put his iPhone away. "I'm glad you're not mad at me anymore."

"Carl, the world doesn't revolve around you."

"I can change. You and I together are better than being apart."

Nina sighed. "I don't want that anymore. It's not important."

Carl looked deflated. "Can't you just give me another chance?"

"You cheated on me, Carl. I don't give second chances on something like that. I said I'd call Jack Reston and I will."

Carl slid out of the booth and came over to hug and kiss her. "Thanks. You're a trouper, Nina. I'm sorry I screwed up."

Nina simply nodded. She just wanted him to go. She

had other things she wanted to think about, like reliving her night with Scott.

She watched Carl leave the dining room and closed her eyes. Why did life have to have so many complications?

Scott didn't expect to see Nina's ex-husband kissing and hugging her when he walked into the dining room. A possessive need to let Carl know Nina was no longer his filled him, but he decided not to intrude. Everything about his relationship with Nina was so new, so tender, that the spark of jealousy that reared up inside him startled him. He backed away and bumped into Hunter.

"You don't look happy," Hunter said.

"I don't want to talk about it."

Hunter just grinned. "Yes, we are." He took Scott by the arm and led him toward the café off the lobby.

Scott ordered coffee and oatmeal. Hunter went for a heartier breakfast of eggs, bacon and toast.

"Why are you here? I thought Lydia's moving into her new house today."

"She is, but I have time for a quick breakfast before I have to collect Maya for the day. Lydia wants her out from underfoot. So what was that face all about?"

"We don't talk about our love lives."

"There's always a first time," Hunter said. "When did you and Nina get a love life?"

The waitress brought mugs and poured coffee into them.

"What makes you think we have a love life?"

"You cooked for her. A man doesn't cook for a woman unless he's serious."

"The problem is I don't know how she feels and just now she was kissing her ex-husband." How could she after last night? He wanted to tell the ex to pack up and go back to LA.

"That ex-husband is a piece of work, but kissing is the Hollywood equivalent of a handshake," Hunter said.

"Why do you say Carl is a piece of work?" Scott hadn't really had a chance to get to know Carl.

"He's demanding, though not in a mean way. He is polite about it, but still he has the staff hopping to make him comfortable. He acts like he's five years old."

"Emotionally, I think he is. I don't know what she saw in him." Scott had been wondering that for a while, but didn't have the courage to ask.

"Lydia told me once her first husband considered her a project. I think maybe that's how Nina viewed Carl, at least according to Kenzie."

"You talked to Kenzie about Nina!" His family was so nosy. How come they never talked to him about stuff?

The waitress brought their food. Scott dug into his oatmeal while Hunter waited for his food to cool.

"Kenzie talked to me about Nina."

"Why?" Scott asked. Kenzie was the youngest and had always confided in him or Donovan. With Donovan so far away, and Scott and Kenzie both on the East Coast only a couple hours away from each other, she'd gotten into the habit of talking to him. Why was she talking to Hunter?

"Honestly, I think Kenzie had a fantasy about you and Nina getting together."

"Tell Kenzie to stay out of my love life," Scott growled.

"Like that's going to happen. Kenzie won't stop until she feels you're settled."

Scott abruptly changed the subject. "What are you and Maya doing today?"

"I'm taking her to the zoo."

"I didn't know Reno had a zoo."

"It's not a big zoo, but I think Maya will enjoy it. She's

really into animals. The other day she tried to talk Nina out of her dog."

"That's not going to happen. Nina loves that dog." Scott wasn't sure he did.

Scott glanced at the lobby and saw Carl strolling toward the casino. Carl wasn't a big gambler, but he did enjoy blackjack. A few minutes later, Nina headed toward the elevators. She stopped at the narrow pond that bisected the lobby and part of the casino. She watched the koi wriggle toward her. No one was supposed to feed the fish, except their keeper, but she tossed crumbs into the water and the koi fought each other for the food. She turned and continued to the elevators.

"I have to get going." Hunter finished his coffee in one gulp. "I'll see you later, bro."

"See ya," Scott replied. He finished his oatmeal and lingered over another cup of coffee before deciding it was time to get to work.

Belle Sampson walked down the path toward Scott. He'd set up an interview with her away from his office as she requested. He wouldn't put it past Gary White or any of his cronies to eavesdrop.

She sat on the bench next to him. Hammering filled the air. The exterior of the spa was up and inside men walked back and forth working on walls and floors.

"That is going to be one nice spa," Belle said.

"Like I would know."

She paused and studied him. "What did you want to talk about? Are you having a problem with my job?"

"Not you. Let me ask you a question. What are the positives of our security department?"

"Um…I…" She sighed.

"I need you to be brutal," Scott said.

She considered his question. "Okay. Cards on the table, no retaliation."

"Yep," Scott replied.

"The visible people have nice uniforms." Despite his urging, her tone was still tentative. "The undercover people blend in nicely."

Scott nodded. "Those are pluses?"

"We have good benefits," she continued, though her gaze wouldn't meet his. "And this place pays pretty well and I have more confidence in management than I used to. Not that Jasper was a negligent owner, but he liked to play and didn't always pay attention to the details."

"By management, do you mean my grandmother or me?"

She paused again as though choosing her words carefully. "Both. You care."

Scott leaned back. "What about things that aren't working?"

"You have a handful of employees who feel entitled and do whatever they want to do."

"Like Gary White and his group."

"They are the ringleaders. They aren't happy because you notice everything."

"That's sort of the point of being an effective security force."

She turned to the side to watch him. "You said brutal and honest."

"Yes."

She took a deep breath. "Gary White has allowed certain…criminal elements to operate in the casino as long as he and his buddies get a kickback."

"Like the pickpockets, the hookers in the bars and the unregistered bookie."

Belle bit the corner of her mouth, worry plain in her

eyes. Scott could see she was struggling with what she wanted to say. "The bookie is Gary's uncle."

"Why didn't you do anything about it?"

"I did. I tried to explain to Jasper what was going on. Jasper talked to Gary, Gary talked to me and I need my job. I have two children and a house payment. And jobs right now aren't exactly easy to find. And things weren't completely intolerable. Mitchel Richards, who headed the security department before you arrived, was a good man. He tried to get the bad ones out. Gary did something and the next thing I knew, Mitch was fired and discredited and he's been looking for a job for the last fourteen months."

"He can't discredit me," Scott said quietly. And he made a note to call the man. Maybe Richards would like a consulting job.

Silence fell between them for a minute and then she said, "So why are we having this conversation?"

"I'm creating a new position, Assistant Director of Security, and you're it."

Surprised, she stared at him, her mouth slightly open. "No. No. I don't believe you. You can't do that, can you?"

"I can do anything I need to do to get security back up to par. And the first thing we're going to do is have everyone recertified on firearms, self-defense classes, and the Secret Service is going to set up workshops because I want to train everyone in the casino on cash handling. Everyone needs to know how to spot counterfeit money, counterfeit debit and credit cards. What about you? Do you have any ideas on areas you'd like to improve?" He knew he was the expert, but he wanted her to feel as though her voice were important.

"Underage drinking is a big problem, especially when parents leave their teenage children unattended. I saw in one of the other hotels refrigerators that can only be opened with a particular type of card. I'd like to see us replace the refrigerators we have with the others. I know that's an expense you may not be able to deliver on, but it could be done in the future. I'd like room service to request an adult's approval when liquor is ordered. I'd like to see more women on the security staff."

She'd already thought about the improvements she wanted to see. "Okay. Those are really good ideas." He'd been so focused on problems that he hadn't noticed the lack of variety on the security force. Having more women was smart. Most victims of crime were women and a woman was more likely to talk to a woman than a man. "Do you want the job?"

She nodded. "When do you want to have all these things in place?"

"Before Thanksgiving. That's the start of the big holiday rush and New Year's Eve is the grand reopening. I'm going to need more security during the holidays especially since my grandmother and Nina Torres have come up with this idea of having someone win a ten-million-dollar jackpot."

"That's going to bring in the riffraff."

"No kidding," Scott said. "We've already had a number of registrations from some of the celebrities Nina invited." And the headaches they would bring. "I have to have a secure casino and hotel in place, ready to go."

"We don't have much time. It's already the middle of September."

"We'll be working fast." He pinched the bridge of his nose. "And putting in a lot of long days. Are you up to it?"

"Yes." New enthusiasm shone in her eyes.

"You'll probably need an assistant. Anybody in mind?"

"You bet. And I can have her here tomorrow. Her name

is Emma McManus. And you'll like her. She's like you—
she takes no prisoners."

Scott chuckled. He'd made the right choice.

Manny Torres had taken over the old chef's office. Lua
el Sol was being run by Nina's eldest brother in his absence
so he could devote time to the hotel restaurant. Like Nina,
Manny loved a challenge. His laptop was open and for a
second Nina wasn't certain who he was talking to. She
leaned over his shoulder and saw he was video-chatting
with Donovan Russell. Her dad was using technology!

Grace stood at the window looking out at the side street.
She held sheet music in her hand, her lips moving as she
read it.

Donovan Russell looked like his brothers but had more
of a pirate look, with a gold earring and black braids pulled
away from his lean face. He owned his own restaurant in
Paris and one of the reasons he was having trouble getting away was because his ex-wife was still trying to get
the financing to buy out his half of their restaurant and he
didn't feel he could leave her in a lurch until he trained his
replacement. He and Manny communicated almost daily
as they worked out the menus for Rio in Reno.

"I tried out the *Vatapá* and served it to a couple of my
customers. They loved it," Donovan said.

Nina loved it, too. Shrimp curry was always a great
meal in her book.

"I emailed you a recipe for *Moqueca de Peixe*," Manny
said. "It's a fish stew and best with grouper, monkfish,
snapper, mahimahi and salmon. It goes well with rice and
fried plantains."

"I love a good fish stew," Donovan replied. He turned
slightly and said something to someone standing behind
the laptop. "Everything seems to be working out well. I'll

try the new recipe and let you know tomorrow." He disconnected and her father sat back to grin at her.

"What brings you to the kitchen?"

Nina sat on the corner of his desk. "I know I'm not the greatest cook in the world, so I need a little help."

Nina intercepted an odd look between her parents. Then her mother ducked her head trying to hide her grin.

"What did you have in mind?"

"I was thinking about *Torta Mousse de Maracujá*."

"Cooking for Scott?" her mother asked.

"He cooked for me last week and I'm reciprocating. You always told me I needed to be polite and appreciate gestures like his." Did she sound pompous or what? She wasn't ready to tell her parents she slept with him. Though she could tell from the look on her mother's face she'd already guessed.

"You want the ingredients, you want help cooking, or do you just want me to make it?" her father asked in an amused tone.

"I want the ingredients. I can cook it myself. It may not turn out as good as yours, but the point is, I want to do it myself." And then she wanted… Her mind shied away from the thoughts of Scott in her bed. Who was she kidding? She wanted to knit him a sweater.

"I can get them for you. I assume you want them now." Manny turned back to his laptop, typed briefly and then the printer started up. A few seconds later, he held his recipe in his hand, scanning it. "I need to hit the market. I have everything but the passion fruit. I'll be back in an hour." He walked out, leaving Nina with her mother.

Her mother snapped her laptop closed and leaned back in her chair. "You've slept with him, haven't you?"

"Do I have a sign on my forehead?" Nina asked, exasperated. She'd never been able to keep secrets from her mother.

Grace grinned. "You've never been very good at hiding your emotions."

Nina collapsed in her dad's empty chair. "I know. I'm never going to be cool like that. My job is to be emotional. People know when a person is faking feelings. I can't promote something if I don't believe in it."

"The way you believed in Carl."

Nina ordered her thoughts. "Until he stopped believing in me."

"Then why is he back?"

"Don't tell me he's bothering you." Nina rubbed her eyes. Her parents had always been ambivalent about Carl. They'd supported her marriage because she was their daughter and that was what they did, but she'd always known they'd never fallen for his charm. Their relationship with Carl had always been cordial because they pretty much got along with everybody, even Carl's high-maintenance parents.

"He's been trying to convince us to help him get you back."

"And how's that going for him?"

Grace burst into laughter. "We picked our side the day you were born, sweetie. Though I have to say, Carl was always generous. Your dad loved the new copper pots Carl gave him and I still love the diamond earrings."

"Carl never did understand how to underplay a role. He equates gifts with favors. Give an expensive something and get a favor back He tried to buy my love."

"He still is."

"Then why did he come here and bring his bimbo with him?" Nina cried in exasperation.

"Because he's not the brightest bulb on the Christmas tree, Nina."

"He's crazy stupid because he sees his career going away and he's panicking."

"He still has a house in Beverly Hills." Grace frowned.

"He's making money hand over fist with the movies he's been doing. One of them turned into a cult movie despite going straight to video."

"In his defense, Nina," her mother said patiently, "you want to bring all the cool people to this casino and he wants to be with the cool people. He wants the cool people to take him seriously."

Nina flinched. Leave it to her mom to give her a reality check. "What's the difference between what Carl wants and what I want? He's making a darn good living with those schlocky movies. I'm only as good as my last job. I know who spends money. Cool people spend their money and that's the dollar I want. Carl burned his bridges in the divorce and he wants to be king of the hill again, but wants me to do all the work." She had to admit she'd liked the lifestyle Carl had provided for her and despite her initial contacts that got him in the door, he'd provided her with a broader group of people to develop contacts with. So she had used him, too.

"What do you think you owe him?" Grace asked in a serious tone.

Nina had to think about that a moment. "Logically, nothing. Emotionally, even less."

"What you want is to get him off your back. What will that take?"

"A three-movie deal from a studio. If he put as much effort into finding his own projects with a major studio than he did into trying to get me to do it for him, he'd have a ten-movie deal from someone." She'd tried to teach him how to get his own big-budget deals, how to schmooze the right people, but he didn't think he needed to know when he had her. "He wants my magic. Pure and simple."

"Are you enjoying stringing him along?"

"I should hope you raised me better than that. A little part of me does enjoy this power Carl has given me, but not enough to abuse it. I'm going to help him, because artistically he does have something to offer."

Grace smiled. "Then get him a three-movie deal. That will keep him occupied for the next ten years."

Nina already knew that. "What I really need to do is find him a Nina, Jr. to marry."

"Do you know anyone who could fill your shoes?"

"I like to think I'm unique." Though the concierge, Celia, had a way with her. She'd taken Carl in hand and gotten him out of Nina's hair. She'd have to think about this.

"Which brings me back to Scott in a roundabout way. You really like him, don't you?"

Nina sighed. "A lot. He's not like the men I normally run into. He's not interested in getting something from me."

"In other words, he just wants to be with you."

"I'm not certain I know how to act with him."

"Sure you do."

Could she really have a relationship with a man like Scott and keep her job? Even though her job was pretty much something she could do anywhere, it still involved a lot of travel. Maybe she was over-thinking this relationship. Maybe he was someone to have fun with and when her job was done she'd just go on to the next one.

"What do you want, Nina?"

"I want to give this hotel and casino a new lease on life. I like being with Scott. He doesn't need me for anything."

"Then maybe it's time to start feeling with your heart and not thinking with your brain."

Nina studied her mother. The years were being kind to her, but she did notice a few lines radiating out from her eyes and the laugh lines around her mouth. "Is that how you felt about Dad when you first met him?"

"Your father bowled me over. After a few dates, I knew he'd always be my best friend and a marriage works a lot better when the partners are friends. I knew I was going to marry him after the second date, but I made him work for it. And here it is thirty-seven years later and I'm more in love with him now than ever before."

Nina wanted that for herself. She wanted a man who overwhelmed her with passion and who would always be her friend. She suspected Scott was that person.

"Thanks, Mom." She kissed Grace on the cheek. "You are the most awesome mother in the world."

Grace hugged her. She'd given Nina a lot to think about.

Nina headed back to her suite. The first thing on her agenda was to call Jack Reston and get Carl that three-movie deal.

The passion fruit pie sat on the counter looking terrific. Nina was proud of her accomplishment. Even though she knew how to cook, she was an indifferent cook. Her busy lifestyle didn't lend itself to long afternoons in the kitchen.

Scott opened a bottle of wine and poured her a glass. "What smells so good in your oven?"

"Food that I cooked. I rarely cook."

"Don't you like to cook?" He handed her the wineglass.

She swirled the red wine around the interior and took a moment to sniff it. "I enjoy cooking, but cooking doesn't enjoy me."

"I'm not quite sure how to interpret that." He'd helped her set the table for dinner.

She opened the small oven and pulled out the casserole. Nothing fancy. "I don't have time to cook. I'd rather knit or garden. One of the things I miss about my old backyard in Beverly Hills is my garden."

"I would never have guessed that gardening and knitting were your hobbies." Scott gave her grin. "You just seem so focused on your career I find it hard to see you in a garden or with knitting needles in your hands."

She uncovered the pot roast casserole and started scooping out the potatoes and carrots. "I can knit anywhere. Except on a plane because the security will take my needles away so I have to pack my gear in my suitcase."

"What do you knit?" He watched as she transferred the pot roast to a cutting board and placed a pan in the stove. She poured the juices from the roast into the pan and turned on the flame.

"Sweaters, scarves, baby booties. Anything that takes my fancy." The booties she knitted for Jack Reston's baby had turned out so beautiful she doubted little Milo would ever wear them.

"How are things going with your ex?"

"I talked to a friend today and they are going to put him in the running for the new superhero franchise they're developing."

"Do you think he'll get the contract?"

Nina thought for a second. "The straight-to-video movies he's been doing are actually a great training ground for a superhero film. They're not that dissimilar, just with a smaller budget and D-list actors. I have to say Carl is pretty imaginative and he did things with those movies that surprised even me."

"I would never think titles like *Shark-A-Conda* would lay the ground for a superhero."

"Hollywood is all about perspective. One of Carl's selling points is that he's great at sticking to a budget, even bringing the movie in under budget. Saving money in Hollywood is almost as good as marrying the boss's ugly daughter."

Scott laughed. "I hope he gets the deal."

"Me, too," Nina said fervently.

A knock sounded at the door and Nina frowned. "Who would that be?"

"You'll to have to answer it to find out." Scott took over at the cutting board, sectioning the pot roast.

Nina gave her gravy a quick stir and lowered the temperature. A series of impatient knocks sounded and she hurried to the door, opened it and stood back as Anastasia burst inside. One look at Scott standing in the dining area with a knife in one hand stopped her. Her mouth fell open.

"Oh," Anastasia said. "I didn't realize you were eating." She turned to Nina. "I need to talk to you about something…private."

Nina glanced at Scott, who raised his eyebrows in surprise. "Scott and I were just about to sit down to dinner." Nina struggled with the next words. "I suppose we can talk…in the bedroom."

Anastasia walked purposely toward the open bedroom door, turned and looked at Nina. "Are you coming?"

Nina followed reluctantly. She didn't really want to know what was on Anastasia's mind. But at the same time, she needed the other woman. Anastasia was a fame magnet. She was always in the press and Nina was able to hitch promotions off her. Having Anastasia in her corner was important. She could deal with Anastasia being Anastasia.

"It's important." Anastasia tapped one foot impatiently. She crossed her arms and waited, one eyebrow raised.

Nina nodded and closed the door. She could hear Scott moving around the kitchen.

"This is a personal matter," Anastasia said.

What did she want? A movie role? A commercial for makeup? Anastasia didn't come here to bond with Nina. "What's wrong?"

"Are you and Scott hooking up?"

Taken aback, Nina didn't have an answer. "We're just having dinner."

"I think it's more than that. You've been on a number of outings with him."

Anastasia was keeping close tabs on her. "We're exploring Reno?" Nina had to tread carefully.

Anastasia flopped down on the edge of the bed. "My daddy has plans for Scott."

Really. Nina felt on the defensive. "What kind of plans?"

"You can't tell anyone this. Promise."

Nina didn't want to promise. "Who would I tell?"

"Promise." Anastasia's eyes narrowed and her body stiffened.

"I won't go to the press with this information if that's what you're worried about."

Anastasia relaxed and patted the bed next to her, but Nina refused, sitting down in a chair instead and crossing her legs. "My daddy is putting together a committee to explore a run for president."

Nina was stunned. The senator liked to deal cheap, fast and easy. In Hollywood that wasn't a bad thing, but in the political arena that made her nervous. "So what does that have to do with Scott?"

"Daddy was never in the military. He wants someone

on his staff who has been, and who has served with honor and distinction. He wants Scott. Daddy trusts him."

Kenzie had never talked a lot about Scott's military career and Nina realized she knew nothing about it except what few things he shared with her, which was almost nothing. "Does Scott know all this?"

"Not yet. You can't be involved with him."

"Why?"

"Nina, your family is in show business."

Show business had a lot of influence in the political arena. "And that's a problem...why?" Being in the entertainment field didn't stop Ronald Reagan from being president, Fred Thompson from being a senator or Arnold Schwarzenegger from being a governor. Nina had been approached a number of times by people in entertainment who wanted to run for office. She didn't do politics because it was messy. "You do realize Scott's grandmother supported her grandchildren by being a professional gambler and for all intents and purposes she was a single mother. Or rather grandmother."

Anastasia sighed as though Nina was being stupid. "Single mothers who raise terrific children are admired and as for being a single grandmother, my daddy could spin that like you wouldn't believe. And as for you, you're a choice...and in Daddy's mind, a bad choice. And Daddy thinks Scott would be a terrific husband for me." She flipped back her hair, raising her chin in a defiant gesture.

Nina was so startled at the last comment that she couldn't focus for a few seconds. "I'm kind of speechless." She was having a hard time imagining Scott married to Anastasia.

Anastasia leaned forward and patted Nina's hand. "Daddy's a real smart man. He knows how to get the votes. And I like Scott. So I need you to back off."

Nina stood up. What she wanted to do was get rid of this

woman. She needed to think. "I will take all of this under advisement." She opened the bedroom door and smiled at Anastasia. "I have dinner waiting." Anastasia raised an eyebrow as though expecting an invitation. Nina walked to the front door and opened it to the hallway. "Thank you, Anastasia, for all your input."

Anastasia hesitated. She glanced at Scott who stood out on the balcony, wineglass in hand. "I'll talk to you later."

"I'll put that on my to-do list." Nina gestured at the door and Anastasia stepped out and turned her mouth open as though to add something. Nina closed the door before any more words could come out. Scott turned at the sound of the door closing. Nina went out to the balcony, accepting her own glass of wine from him as he waited leaning against the balcony.

"What did she want?" Scott asked curiously.

Nina wondered what to tell him. She hadn't promised not to say anything to Scott; she'd only promised to keep her knowledge out of the press.

Finally, she said, "We need to talk." She gave him every piece of detail Anastasia had told her and watched as his face changed from being relaxed and calm to closed and emotionless. "I'm hungry, but I'm skipping dinner and going right to the dessert."

Scott didn't say anything. Nina went back inside to cut the *Torta Mousse de Maracujá.* Scott stopped her. "No. A proper meal first." He put the pot roast on the table and pulled out a chair for Nina.

She wanted to ask him what he was thinking, but found herself, probably for the first time in her life, at a loss for words. They ate in silence. Scott's face was closed and remote and Nina could tell he was thinking really hard.

With his plate finally empty, Scott pushed back from the table. He cleaned his plate into the garbage disposal and put it into the dishwasher. Nina did the same. With dessert plates in hand, they went to sit on the balcony.

"You haven't said a word." Nina watched him closely.

"Oh, hell, no."

"To what?" she asked.

"To all of it."

"But…"

"I thought about this during this wonderful meal you cooked me and I know I don't want to have anything to do with Senator Parrish. That man is shady and that's me being polite."

"I was thinking more along the lines of morally bankrupt, but I'll go with shady," Nina said. She took a bite of the *Torta Mousse de Maracujá*. Heavenly.

Scott stared out at the night sky. "Senator Parrish is the kind of man who expects a person to do hard time for him. He wants a hatchet man."

"Do you really think so?" She didn't trust the senator either.

"I know so. He has access to my military records."

"Tell me," Nina coaxed.

"No." His tone was firm.

"What happens now?" She had had a hard time getting out of working for Senator Parrish. She'd been in the middle of her divorce and the senator had been relentless in his desire for her to work for him. She had considered hiding in Fiji to escape.

"Let's put it on hold, I have something else in mind right now."

She raised an eyebrow. "Really. What?"

He grinned, pulled her into his arms and ran his fingers over her breasts.

"That's what you have in mind."

"Objection?" he asked.

"None at all."

He lifted her in his arms and carried her to the bedroom. Desire pooled inside her. She was on a roller coaster of excitement and she liked the thrill that vibrated through her.

Scott set her on her feet at the side of the bed. Her legs were so wobbly she lost her balance. Her throat went dry. Unable to look away, she watched him remove his tie, ball it up and stick it in his pocket. Then he slipped his jacket off and draped it over the chair. He was stripping for her. How exciting, she thought, and found herself smiling in anticipation.

"Nina." He started to unbutton his white shirt.

She raised her head and his eyes met hers. "Do you want me to get undressed now?"

"It's a great dress, but I'd like to see it on the floor."

Nina thought his request a bit odd, but it also sounded sexy. Carl had never made her feel sexy the way Scott did. "If that's what you want."

"It is."

Nina pulled off her dress and headed toward the closet.

"What are you doing?" he asked curiously.

"This is a Dolce and Gabbana. I can't toss it on the floor."

His chest rumbled as if he was trying not to laugh. "Really?"

"It's couture."

Scott snatched the dress out of her hand and tossed it on the rug. "I'll pick it up later."

Normally she liked being the bossy one, but from Scott she found it incredibly exciting. She swallowed her response and reached behind her and unhooked her bra. She pulled it off and let it dangle from her fingers before letting it fall on top of her dress.

He grabbed her wrist and brought her hand to his very hard penis. "This is what you do to me."

Nina felt his hard length against her palm. He was so strong and so powerful. Her heart began racing. Heat gushed between her legs.

"This is why I can't wait," he whispered.

Her mouth opened and closed. She wasn't certain she could speak.

"I need you." Scott cupped her breast and gently kneaded it.

"Yes," she moaned. "Me, too." This was how it was supposed to feel like between a man and woman.

"Good." Scott reached into his pocket and pulled out a row of condoms. He ripped one off the row and tossed the rest on the bed.

The white packets were stark against the olive-and-burgundy fabric of the duvet cover. One corner of his mouth quirked up in a smile as if he'd just thrown down a gauntlet. Did he think she was going to be that easy? She stared at his beautiful sculpted chest, admiring his muscles, his everything. She watched him take off his shoes and socks, and then he stood and unbuckled his belt. Scott unzipped his pants, dropped them on the floor and quickly put the condom on. "Take down your hair."

Nina stared at his engorged penis. Soon that would be inside her. Her breath came in short, heavy pants at the thought of him inside her. She began to tremble.

"Nina."

She raised her eyes to his face. His nostrils were flared. "Yes?"

"Take down your hair."

Nina reached up and took the mother-of-pearl hair combs out and let the heavy weight of her hair fall free. She put the combs on the night table. As she turned around, he grabbed her around the waist and lifted her up. "Wrap your legs around me."

Nina did as commanded. He lowered her until she lay on her back. Without giving her any time to think, he knelt between her legs.

"You are so beautiful. You are the most delicious looking woman, in and out of your clothes." His tone was teasing, but the seriousness in his eyes told her how much he desired her.

He slid two fingers inside her, circling her inner muscles. Pleasure curled through her. Dear God, she was ready to explode. The calloused pad of his thumb moved slowly over her hard bud. Nina couldn't seem to catch her breath. He moved faster, harder, driving her to the edge.

He withdrew his fingers and gently used her wetness on her nipples. She strained forward. He teased her breasts, cupping them and then blowing gently on the engorged nipples. They grew even tighter.

She clutched at him, trying to draw him down on top of her, but he gave her a teasing grin and lowered his mouth to her cleft, his tongue expertly taking over for his thumb. She gasped. Pleasure rode her in waves. Her hips rose frantically.

He tenderly teased her skin, moving up over her stomach to her waist, her ribs, to her breasts with his tongue and fingers. Her inner muscles clenched with the need for fulfillment. His erection pushed against her inner lips while he continued to suckle, nibble and swirl his tongue around her nipples. He lowered himself, the tip of his penis gently pushing inside.

His face was tight with tension. His eyes squeezed shut.

"Scott?"

"You feel so good."

Nina wriggled her hips trying to get him farther inside her, wrapping her legs tightly around him.

His mouth found hers, his tongue at first gentle, then harder on hers. A shuddering breath escaped her. The feel of him so deep inside left her breathless, building toward her climax. He pulsed inside her.

Suddenly he stopped and pulled back slightly.

"Don't stop," she moaned.

"I'm not." He rolled on his back and with his hands on her waist, he pulled her up on him. He grinned at her.

She froze, uncertain how to continue. Carl never liked her on top. "I don't… I never…"

He put a finger against her mouth. "Hush. I have you."

Nina spread her hands over his hard nipples and braced herself. She could feel him pulsing so deeply inside her she couldn't breathe. He slid his hands to her hips, his fingers spread across her butt cheeks. Slowly, he guided her hips up and down. He filled her so completely, so deeply, her muscles spasmed with desire.

"So good. You feel so…good." Nina braced her knees on either side of his hips and fell into the rhythm of his hands as they guided her. She moved up and down, grinding onto him to pull him even more deeply into her. One hand reached between them to rub her clitoris. The other hand reached for her nipple.

Her orgasm began to build. Her muscles clenched against the friction. His fingers on her nub added to the passion spiraling out of control. He thrust hard into her and her desire escalated until she started to explode in her climax and she could feel his own orgasm in tune with hers.

She couldn't breathe, she couldn't think. She strained against him until they both went over the edge.

Chapter 9

Nina called Carl and asked him to meet her at the café for lunch. She found him already sitting in a booth, looking nervous. She sat down on the opposite bench, pushing her tote into the corner. The waitress, having gotten to know Nina's tastes, brought her an iced tea and Nina politely thanked her.

Carl gave her an expectant look, hope in his eyes. "Well."

She reached into her tote and pulled out a plane ticket. She slid the plane ticket across the table. He reached for it, but she refused to let go. "Your plane leaves for LA in three hours. You remember Tasha, my stylist? She will pick you up and take you home. She's going to go through your closet and lay out what you are going to wear and where you are going to wear it. She'll start with the clothes for your dinner meeting with Jack tomorrow night. Right now, you look desperate and you smell desperate." She put two scripts in front of him. "Jack is going to give you a chance to sell yourself. But…" she paused long enough to make sure he was listening to her "…everything is dependent on your being able to direct two episodes of *Sunset Cop*."

His face twisted into disdain. "That show is stupid."

"It's number twelve in the ratings and that's respectable enough, but the show can do better. You're going to read these scripts and come up with some dynamite ideas to make this show number one. And then you will sell Jack your ideas."

Carl took the scripts. "Then what?"

"If he's happy with your work and the numbers are decent, he'll give you a shot at the movie you want." She handed him a third script thicker than the first two. "I was able to get this for you so you can study it and come up with ideas. It's still in draft and there will be a few more changes, but it will give you an idea of what the movie is about."

He eagerly grasped the script. "Is that all?"

"No. *Sunset Cop* is over budget and the star is threatening to walk off the set if the scripts don't improve because he's a prima donna who thinks he's bigger than the show. This is your chance and I worked hard to get this opportunity for you. Bring it in under budget, which I know you can do, and you're going to make Lenny Hodges your best friend. Make him happy to be the star of *Sunset Cop*. If you can do all this, Jack will give you a second meet to discuss *Star Chaser*. Impress Jack. Make him want you not because I got you this chance, but because you are the right person for this movie."

"Did you read *Star Chaser*?"

"I did. I'm going to be honest—this script still needs a lot of work. It's already gone through four rewrites." She paused as the waitress set her BLT in front of her. She leaned forward, looking directly into Carl's eyes so he would understand her next words. "This is the last time I will do something like this for you, Carl."

He closed his eyes and took a deep breath. "Why did I ever let you go?"

"You didn't let me go. Your ego pushed me out."

He took her hand. "I'm sorry, Nina. I was stupid."

"I could have fought for you," she replied. "But I didn't. We both are at fault."

"I'm not good at saying thank-you, or admitting I was wrong."

"Carl," she said. "That's the best apology you've ever given me. Now get out of here. Land this job and be happy. And find a good woman who isn't a bimbo." She pushed out of the booth and left Carl paging though the first of the two *Sunset Cop* scripts, his lunch forgotten. "Don't screw up. Like I said, I'm not doing this again for you."

In the lobby, she found Scott talking with Gary White. The man stood rigidly, hands tensed at his side while Scott talked. Abruptly Gary nodded and walked off without a backward glance.

"What was that all about?" she asked.

"He's not happy about the changes I've made." Scott watched the man walk through the lobby doors to the outside.

"He's on your list, I take it."

"Yes," Scott replied. "So what are you doing for dinner tonight?"

"Hopefully you."

He looked taken aback and then burst into laughter. "I'm in. How about dinner first, though."

"Are you cooking?"

"Let's have a date. Dinner and a show. You pick the place."

Nina smiled. "An old friend of my parents' is performing with his band at the Cowboy Palace."

"Who?"

"T.J. March."

"The country-western singer! Didn't he just win a CMA?"

"He did, for his album *Hello, Country.* My mom sang backup."

"Your mom seems to know everybody."

"She's been in the business for years and occasionally does session work." If Nina had had one ounce of talent, she would have followed her mom into the music business.

"I'm game, but country-western isn't at the top of my list."

"You'll love T.J. He's got a touch of blues, some rockabilly and little bit of rock. And if you're really, really nice tonight, I'll introduce you."

He kissed her on the cheek just as Carl entered the lobby. He took one look at Scott and his eyebrows arched. He gave Nina a friendly wave and headed to the elevators. She offered up a tiny prayer that Carl did what needed to be done to assure his future. She wanted the best for him.

"I'll meet you here in the lobby around seven." Scott headed toward the casino and Nina went to the elevator. She had work to do, though she couldn't stop smiling, remembering the feel of Scott's lips on her cheek.

A valet took Scott's SUV and he ushered Nina into The Blue Velvet restaurant. She looked stunning yet funky in a red dress bordered with black. It reminded him of a flapper's dress from the Roaring Twenties. She wore black spike heels on her narrow feet that added enough height that she was almost nose to nose with him. She'd pulled her hair straight back from her face and secured her hair with crystal-encrusted barrettes. She looked delicious.

The inside of The Blue Velvet was dim and quiet. Booths lined the walls and the waitress led them to one in a shadowed corner. Nina slid in and Scott followed her. The table was rounded on the inside and he could sit next to her breathing in the delicate, floral scent of her perfume.

She leaned into him, her body warm and inviting. His libido went into impatient overdrive as he thought about how their evening would end.

"Welcome to The Blue Velvet," their waiter said. "Have you eaten here before?"

"No," Scott answered.

"Then you are in for a treat. We have no menu. The chef decides what he wants to cook and we serve only the one dish until it is gone. Tonight's offering is Beef Wellington. It is paired with a slightly fruity red wine from a local vineyard. Enjoy your meal."

"That was interesting," Nina said, watching the waiter leave for another table where he repeated his lecture.

"We're on an adventure here," Scott said, taking her hand.

She murmured agreement and leaned into him more closely. The candlelight from the table reflected in her eyes and his breath caught in his throat. She was the sexiest, most beautiful woman he'd ever known.

"I see Carl checked out. I'm assuming he's on his way to Los Angeles for his new life."

Nina nodded with a happy smile. "Free at last."

He minded having Carl around, and felt awkward at times while talking to her ex-husband. "Why help him? He's not your problem anymore."

"He was my problem. I took over so much of his life and ran it for him, he didn't know how to take charge for himself. Talent alone isn't enough to be successful in Hollywood. You've lived in Washington, DC. That's a tougher town than Hollywood any day."

"Living in DC is all about compromise. I didn't know how much I hated it until my grandmother won that poker game."

"Then why stay? You could have work anywhere."

"My best army buddy, Danny, started the business and asked me to help get it off the ground. I did that. I gave him three years. The business is thriving and I needed to move on."

"If Anastasia has her way…"

"She won't. Her father is the kind of man you sell your soul to, and I'm not selling."

"I already know that, but does Anastasia know? She is a woman on a crusade."

"I have to convince her that what she wants and what her father wants isn't going to happen." Scott liked his new life. He wasn't going back.

"I'm going to tell you that saying no to the senator is like putting a bullet in your own brain."

"I know where a few bodies are buried."

"Ones you're connected to?" Nina asked curiously.

"No." He was tired of dirty deals and backroom politics. "My future is working for my family. At first, I thought my grandmother was insane, but I've discovered she's the smartest cookie in the box."

"She is that. Miss E. is amazing. And so is Lydia. Neither one blinked about the ten-million-dollar jackpot. I wasn't expecting them to be so comfortable or open-minded about it."

The waiter returned with bread rolls. "The rolls are salt-crusted sweet bread baked on site especially for our guests and are accompanied by honey butter and apple butter." The sommelier stepped forward holding a bottle of wine that he uncorked in front of them. "The wine," the waiter continued, "is a lovely Cabernet Sauvignon from the Ripe Vine vineyards, a winery right here in the Reno area."

The sommelier poured a little wine into a large, round goblet. Scott swirled the wine in the glass and then gently sipped it. The bouquet was fruity and tart, but he was sure it was perfect. He nodded and the sommelier poured wine into Nina's glass and then more into his own. The waiter and the sommelier withdrew discreetly.

Scott loved this restaurant with its subdued atmosphere and unobtrusive waitstaff. It was made even better by Nina sitting at his side. He just wasn't sure how he could entice her to stay longer.

As Nina nibbled on the bread, her eyes went wide. "Wow. I need to steal one of these rolls for my dad." She broke it apart and put a dab of apple butter on one piece and honey butter on the other and tried each one with a sip of water in between. "This is amazing."

Scott tried a roll as well and was impressed. "Make sure Donovan gets one, too."

"I should have brought a bigger purse." She laughed.

They fell into comfortable silence.

"I need to make a trip to the restroom," Nina said, sliding out of the booth.

Scott watched her as she strolled around the tables, her body swaying gently, the red dress catching the candlelight from the different tables. She was exquisite and the thought of how the night would end made his heart pound so loudly he was certain the whole dining room could hear.

He wanted a relationship with Nina. For the first time in his life, he had the chance to settle down and explore his goals. While in the army he'd been busy doing things he couldn't talk about. As a security specialist with his friend, his life had seldom been his own and now that he had the time, he was becoming involved with a woman who couldn't sit still. At times, he could feel her mind racing, feel her constantly developing ideas. He was totally unprepared for Hurricane Nina and he prided himself on being prepared for everything.

"As I was walking back I saw something interesting,"

Nina said when she returned to the table. "Isn't that your security guard, Gary White, at ten o'clock?"

Scott carefully glanced in the direction she indicated. He could just make out Gary's profile and he frowned. "Yes, that's Gary. He's with Louisa Biggins. Her father, Jasper, originally owned the Casa de Mariposa."

"Call me cynical, but doesn't that seem odd to you?" Nina surreptitiously glanced over her shoulder.

Scott shook his head. "Maybe they're dating."

Nina tilted her head. "If I were as beautiful and rich as she is, he is not the man I would choose to date."

"Nina, are you a snob?"

"I'm realistic. Rich and pretty means you get to be the one who picks."

"But you are rich and pretty."

"And look who I chose," she said, fluttering her eyelashes at him.

Scott chuckled. "You're making me feel like a car."

"Yes, a beautiful, American muscle car. Powerful. In control. Fast. Sleek. Who wants a Bentley when I can have you parked in my driveway?"

"Now that I'm all blushing and hot," Scott said, "we're just having fun, right? You and me."

She paused. "Are we? I thought…"

"Where are we going, Nina?"

She studied him for a moment before answering. "I don't know. Where do you think we should go? I kind of like what we have."

Scott wanted more, but he was not the kind of man to make a decision like this until he knew what she wanted. He wasn't the kind of man to step into a minefield without seeing a path. Nina wasn't a minefield, but the path he saw was littered with complications. She was totally focused on her career and very good at what she did.

One of the most attractive things about her was that she didn't need a man to feel complete. She stood on her two feet and looked the world right in the eye. If she didn't like what she saw, she changed it. She'd carved a career for herself out of nothing. She took some basic organizing skills and people skills and turned it into something really interesting. She was going to rebuild the Casa de Mariposa and her efforts would spill over and revive the whole town. In twenty years, Reno could easily rival Las Vegas and everything would point back to her.

"What are you thinking?" she asked, breaking him out of his reverie.

"I'm trying to figure out what you want."

"Personal and professional? They aren't the same thing."

"Both."

The waiter appeared briefly to refill their wineglasses and announce dinner was on its way. Scott nodded politely and turned his attention back to Nina while she seemed to be searching for an answer.

"Professionally, I want to do good work. I want to help my clients maximize their vision. I want them to be happy doing what they're doing and make money."

Scott could accept that. "What do you want personally?"

She thought a little longer. "I want to be queen of my own destiny."

"I understand that. I've been at the beck and call of other people for the last twelve years. First in the army and then in security. I'm ready to take charge of myself, too."

She smiled at him, reaching for his hand and running her fingers across the inside of his wrist. "When I was a child, my parents made my decisions. When I was married to Carl everything was about him. Now that I'm just me,

I'm looking for the next phase in my life. The problem is I don't know what it is." She sipped her wine.

"I know you'll find your way."

"I know I will, too."

The waiter arrived with a tray holding the plates of food. He set each one carefully down, wished them enjoyment of their meal, and subtly faded back into the shadows.

Scott watched Nina cut into the Beef Wellington. A look of surprise crossed her face and she grinned. "This is good."

"I agree." Scott noticed that Gary White and Louisa Biggins were standing up, their meal finished. Gary draped a shawl around the woman's shoulders and they walked out. Their waiter bowed politely to them, but they ignored him. Scott couldn't help wondering what the two of them were doing. Somehow their meal didn't seem like romance—more like business. He put that thought into the back of his head to examine later.

The Cowboy Palace was bright and garish with neon lights that blinked on and off at a frantic pace. The theater was round with a stage in the center. Nina and Scott had front row seats. Scott was impressed. When T.J. walked onto the stage he saw Nina, waved and blew her a kiss.

The concert was perfect. T.J. knew how to draw in his audience and give them a show. Afterward, T.J. invited Nina and Scott backstage. Scott was thrilled.

T.J.'s dressing room was unassuming and Spartan. No star treatment here. Nina and T.J. embraced and Nina introduced Scott. Scott was a little awed by this quiet man. He was tall and lanky and dressed in faded jeans, a plaid shirt and fancy-stitched cowboy boots that looked a little worn around the edges. He shook hands with Scott, his grip strong and callused.

T.J. offered bottled water to Nina and Scott. Scott twisted the top off the bottle. Nina set hers on the table.

"How are your parents?" T.J. said, sitting down on a sofa.

"They're in town," Nina replied. "They would have come tonight, but Dad is catering a private party and Mom is providing the music. Go on over later, they'll be up and delighted to see you." She gave T.J. directions to the hotel. She started telling him about her job and the New Year's Eve party. In five seconds, T.J. agreed to be a part of the entertainment.

Scott was amazed and suddenly he understood how Nina worked. She had a way of making a person feel incredible. She listened to every word and made suitable comments. Scott sat back and watched. By the time T.J. March let them go, Scott was hooked.

In the car on the way back to the hotel, Scott said, "You had every intention of getting T.J. March to come to play for New Year's Eve at the hotel before you even arrived at the show."

She gave him an innocent look. "I don't know what you're talking about."

Scott chuckled. "I'm really starting to understand you and I...I like you."

Nina grinned. "Stick with me. I'll make sure you have a lot of fun."

"I already am."

Nina didn't know why she'd been invited to what appeared to be an intimate family get-together in Hunter Russell's suite. She was just happy dinner wasn't being served in Miss E.'s RV.

Hunter's suite looked very similar to hers, only much larger with two bedrooms and a bath on one side of the living area and a master suite on the other side with the kitchen tucked in behind the bathroom. Like her suite, double doors opened to a balcony overlooking the pool. Once the whole family figured out if they were going to live on site or find other accommodations, Nina could see these special suites as a terrific draw as family rooms.

Caroline Fairchild bustled about the dining area setting plates on the table while Nina uncorked wine bottles. The spicy aroma from the covered dishes delivered from the kitchen revealed her father had done the cooking.

Lydia came in looking radiant in a lovely summer dress of yellow and white. Maya wore a matching yellow skirt and white blouse. Nina had brought Kong just for Maya to play with. The second Maya found Kong, she immediately picked him up and took him out of the way to play with him.

Scott uncovered dishes and placed them on the table.

Nina found herself off to the side watching Lydia and Hunter. They looked happy as they held hands. Nina wanted what they had and didn't know it until this moment. She glanced at Scott who bent over Miss E., laughing at something she said. She caught part of the conversation as Miss E. apologized for Jasper being unable to attend because of a prior commitment.

Nina felt odd watching everyone, seeing them so happy and relaxed. She'd never been one to envy other people's good fortune, but she had the feeling she was missing something. Something important.

Here she was, only two years away from being thirty, and she'd already accomplished so much. Scott had asked her what she wanted and the question stayed with her while she tried to answer it.

What did she want? She wished she knew. For the first

time since she'd been ten years old, she didn't have a clear goal in front of her. She felt adrift for not knowing.

Nine tried to analyze why she was feeling the way she was. She noticed Scott watching her, a curious look on his face.

Hunter handed out glasses of wine to everyone but Maya, who received grape juice. He called for everyone's attention. Scott came to stand with Nina and she leaned into him enjoying the warmth of his body against her.

"Everyone, can I have your attention," Hunter said holding up a hand.

Conversation died away.

Lydia looked happy as she gazed at Hunter. "We have an announcement to make." The two shared a smile.

"We've decided to get married and we would like to do so on New Year's Day."

Everyone burst into applause. Nina clapped just as enthusiastically while turning over in her mind all the planning that would need to be done. They only had a couple months.

"Nina," Lydia said, "I know you have a lot on your plate, but do you know someone who can help with the planning?"

"Of course, I know several somebodies. I'll get on the phone and call them and see who is available to make your wedding happen. But I need to ask some questions."

"After dinner," Lydia said, "Hunter and I will sit down with you."

Nina nodded. Hunter ushered people toward the dining table and got them seated.

"Can I be your flower girl?" Maya could barely sit still.

"Of course," Lydia replied.

Food made its way around the table. Nina took double helpings. The roast looked deceptively simple, but she knew her father would have packed a lot of surprise flavors in it.

Nina glanced around the table. Next to her, Scott reached under the table to squeeze her hand. She returned the squeeze. Watching this family work reminded her of her family and how moments like this made her feel as though she were a part of something special.

"What's going on with you, Scott?" Miss E. said. "I heard some rumbles about the new security procedures you're putting into place."

Scott buttered a roll. "Not to say anything mean about Jasper, but a few things needed to be overhauled."

Hunter laughed. "Bro, that was very diplomatic. I'm proud of you."

Scott glared at his brother and Nina hid a smile, trying not to laugh. Watching them was just the same as watching her own brothers bicker and tease each other.

"Everyone is being recertified in weapons. I have several workshops we're doing in conjunction with the Secret Service about spotting counterfeit money, and martial arts mastery is also on the table." Scott glanced around. "We're not dealing with terrorists here, but ordinary people who get caught up in unusual circumstances and the security people need to know how to walk the fine line between keeping guests safe and still allowing them to have fun. And all this needs to be an unobtrusive as possible."

Miss E. laughed. "Maybe I should hire a psychiatrist to help with that."

Nina chuckled. "That might not be a bad idea."

"You're kidding," Scott said.

"No, I'm not. You're making sweeping changes to the way things worked before. Even I can see some of the resentment building in some of the employees, especially employees who have been working here for years. They're afraid they're going to lose their jobs. They're confused about the new rules and regulations. People always feel uncomfortable with change, but change happens."

"We're in the business of business," Hunter said.

"And that means, you have to constantly reinvent yourself to stay current." Nina nodded in agreement. "You'll be able to take the momentum from my promotional campaigns for a couple years, and then you'll have to come up with something new."

Miss E. reached over and patted Nina's hand. "That's why I have you, dear."

Nina felt flattered. She hadn't even finished this promotion and Miss E. was already giving her the next one.

"And that constantly affects security." Scott speared meat from the platter. "Because people come up with new and exciting ways to cheat with new scams, new ways of trying to beat the house and just new everything."

"That's progress," Nina said with a laugh. "Progress isn't always fun."

"I can put a positive spin on this," Scott added. "Job security."

Everyone broke out into laughter.

"Who knew," Miss E. said, "such a simple thing like winning a poker game could result in so much chaos and complications."

"And you're enjoying every minute of it," Hunter said.

"I'm sorry Jasper isn't here, but I'm sort of glad." Scott poured gravy over his meat. "Nina and I saw his daughter, Louisa, at The Blue Velvet last week. She was having dinner with one of my people." He'd tried to talk to Gary about the meal he'd shared with Louisa, but Gary hadn't been forthcoming, leaving Scott with a mild sense of unease.

"Louisa wasn't happy about Jasper's decision to get rid of the casino," Miss E. said, her voice troubled.

"Is she someone I need to worry about?" Scott asked.

Miss E. frowned. "I don't know. Louisa wasn't particularly interested in the casino originally. She enjoyed the privileges and the perks that came with being Jasper's only child. When all that was taken away, it's like she lost a part of her identity."

Nina remembered the fierce, pinched look of anger on Louisa's face while she sat with Gary. Louisa was a woman who felt she was entitled to what Jasper could give her. Nina saw a lot of that sense of entitlement in the entertainment industry. Actors, at the top of their game, believed they were more than special, that they could do what they wanted when they wanted. But the reality was they were only one good scandal away from losing everything.

"It must be difficult for Louisa to give up the attention," Nina said, "the ingratiating way other people treated her."

"Maybe," Miss E. conceded, "but Jasper is enjoying his life and loving the fact that he's not responsible for taking care of this place anymore. He settled a trust fund on his ex-wives and his daughter, and is loving this new sense of freedom."

But that wasn't Nina's point. Louisa needed to feel special. "I see time and time again in Hollywood where celebrities claim to hate the attention and publicity, but will pull stunts designed to do nothing but focus attention on them." Maybe Nina could introduce Louisa to some director who might cast her in something. She had the right look and attitude.

"Don't feel sorry for Louisa," Miss E. said gently. "In her head, she might feel she's fallen from grace, but she landed on a big old feather mattress."

"But that doesn't explain," Scott interjected, "why she was having dinner with Gary White."

"Maybe they're dating," Lydia said with a fond look at Hunter. Hunter grinned back at her.

Yeah, Nina thought, they were totally in love and wanted others to share in their glow. "Nope, they didn't have the dating body language, not even the fake dating body language."

Lydia asked, "What, pray tell, is fake dating body language?" She leaned forward gazing at Nina curiously.

"We call it PR dating. Celebrities date to call attention to themselves, or a project they're working on, or to divert the public's attention from something they're hiding, or the 'I'm not gay' date." A lot of celebrities had come out of the closet, but just as many hadn't. "I set up several fake dates myself. Fake dates are terrific publicity. Almost as good as having a baby or a lavish wedding you know is doomed to fail before the two parties finish their vows. And babies are really big business for celebrities."

"How are babies big business?" Lydia asked curiously.

"Babies are publicity platinum, especially for women," Nina replied. "There's the 'I can't wait to see the baby bump' response. How is she dressing the baby bump? If she's not married, who's the baby's daddy? And then afterward, there's whole getting back into shape, who's watching the baby, baby photos, what kind of loot did you get. You have eighteen months of publicity madness."

"What do you give to new mothers?" Miss E. asked.

"I knit baby booties," Nina said. "I'm constantly amazed at the number of expensive gifts new mothers get they can't even use, but my booties are popular and practical. It's that personal touch. Anyone can call Tiffany's and order something and I give something handmade to people who can afford the best of everything. I get pregnancy confirmation before the press. One of my friends told me that my booties are a sign of 'you made it.' People compete for my booties." She'd even had little tags that she put on the booties that said, *Made by Nina, just for you.*

"That's just odd," Lydia said. "If I get pregnant, will you knit a pair for me?"

"I've been waiting for the Russell family to start producing so I can provide booties for them."

Lydia smiled. She exchanged another intimate look with Hunter that excluded everyone at the table except Maya who clapped. "I want a baby brother."

Nina grinned. "Trust me, sweetie, brothers are overrated. I have five of them. They get mad when you dress them up, they don't want you to play with their toys and they rip the heads off your Barbie dolls."

Maya frowned. "I want a sister, instead."

"I'll make that happen," Hunter said with a laugh.

"What are we going to do about Louisa?" Miss E. asked.

"I'm going to keep an eye on her and Gary," Scott said.

Everyone nodded at Scott's comment and the conversation turned back to the wedding.

Nina sat back and watched the family dynamics. She loved being with them. As much as she loved her family, the chaos level with the Russells was so much lower and easier to manage. She settled back and just watched, her mind busy with wedding planners and the New Year's Eve celebration. So much to do and time was slipping away from her.

Chapter 10

Scott knocked on the door to Nina's suite. She flung the door open and gasped when she saw him.

"What is going on?" he asked. She'd left a message in his office to come see her as soon as possible. He'd left his phone in the charger and hadn't had a chance to get back to his suite to grab it. His morning had been ultra-busy with the construction people in the casino building the last step of the viewing case for the ten-million-dollar jackpot. Already the jackpot had generated a ton of new business in the casino for people who wanted a glimpse of what ten million dollars looked like even though the money wasn't in the case yet.

She grabbed his hand. "Come here. You have to see this." She dragged him to her laptop open on the dining table. She pushed him down on the chair. "Look at this." She tapped a key.

All Scott saw was a tangle of legs and arms along with melodramatic groans and tiny gasps. He couldn't make any sense of it. "What am I looking at?"

She pointed at the screen. "Wait for it."

His brain finally sorted out two people rolling around on a bed and then a light went on. He was looking at a sex tape. A sex tape starring…Anastasia Parrish and Nina's ex-husband, Carl Durant!

He leaned closer to the screen, not believing he was seeing what he was seeing.

His first comment was, "Is that really Carl? What is he doing with Anastasia?" The sex part was obvious, but why? "She's ten years younger than he is." His second thought was that her father was going to kill her or put her in a convent. His third thought was that Senator Richard Parrish, who ran on a family values platform, was going to be unemployed come the next election when his very conservative South Carolina constituency saw this.

He turned to Nina. "How did you get this?"

"A friend sent it to me. It was posted this morning."

"This is not good." His thoughts turned to the damage this could do to the hotel. There was no denying that the tape had been made here. The background showed the Casa de Mariposa colors and distinctive furnishings. The date at the bottom said the tape had been filmed several days ago. At the bottom of the screen *Casa de Mariposa* flashed letting the world know where the tape had been done. Scott tried not to groan.

"I can spin this," Nina said with a wave of her hand.

"What about Carl's new start on his career?"

Nina laughed. "This will put him on the radar of every studio in the country. Better than having a baby." Her eyes gleamed. "I know Anastasia probably did this herself, but still I have to ask myself why."

"To embarrass her father," Scott said.

"Most likely, though all she has to do is wake up in the morning to do that. I think this is for you to show you what you're missing."

Scott blinked.

Her phone rang. She glanced at it and sent the call to voice mail.

"But a sex tape!" Scott stared unbelievingly at the screen. "Why?"

"I'm going to be a pop psychiatrist for a moment. You stood up to her father and you stood up to her."

"The man is not that impressive." The senator had a smug, superior manner that grated on him. He felt sorry for Anastasia. She was confused, angry and hurt, which was a dangerous combination.

"He swings his power around like a bat and he doesn't care who it hits as long as he gets what he wants. He's not above using his daughter to further his agenda. So, yes, she is getting back at him while showing you the bonus you could have had. But I'm just speculating. I'm surprised she hasn't done one before."

Incredulously, Scott watched Anastasia twisting herself into the weirdest position he'd ever seen. He tilted his head trying to figure out what was going on. He couldn't believe he was watching this.

Nina's phone rang again. Again, she sent the call to voice mail. A second later it rang again.

"Aren't you going to answer that?"

Her phone rang again. "This one I have to answer. It's Carl." She pressed the talk button. "Hello, Carl, what can I do for you?" She listened, a smile on face growing. "Sex tape? Heavens. How did something like that ever happen?"

Carl's voice was an indistinct murmur. Whatever he was saying amused Nina. At one point she covered her mouth to keep from laughing. "Carl, you know how to spin this. Own it. People are going to think you're hot stuff. A senator's daughter. This is one promotion that was made in heaven. How could you not know Anastasia was filming the two of you?" She listened again. "You'll be fine. Just own it. I have to go. I'll talk to you later."

She disconnected and doubled over laughing.

"You think this is funny." Scott did, too, but wondered what Nina found so amusing.

"Yes. Don't you?"

"Yes, it's amusing. Carl sounded upset." Carl hadn't come across to Scott as someone who would do something like this. Deep down inside, Carl was a private person and even though Scott didn't particularly like him, he was, in his own way, a nice enough man.

"For about thirty seconds, until he realized this is great for his career."

"How is this good for his career?"

"He's with a senator's daughter who is almost as media savvy as me. She knows how to get her name out there and now Carl's name is linked with hers. This is awesome. Notoriety in Hollywood is golden. Only a few things trump a sex tape."

"Such as…" Scott coaxed.

"A good stint in rehab."

"Your world is messed up," Scott said.

"I'm inclined to agree. Everyone loves a good failure. The only people who aren't allowed to fail are people like me. I have to knock the ball out of the park every time. But actors, directors, writers fall on their faces all the time and rise like a Phoenix from the ashes. The public watches them struggle to regain themselves and feels like they're a part of their lives."

"But not everyone pulls themselves back up." Scott could think of a number of celebrities who disappeared into obscurity after particularly nasty failures.

"Then we get to feel superior." Nina turned the laptop to look at the screen.

"The senator isn't going to like this."

"I know. He's already called me…" she looked at her

phone, which she had turned to vibrate "...seventeen times. I'm surprised he hasn't called you."

"I left my phone on the charger this morning and haven't had time to get it. Besides, I'm not her babysitter, no matter how much the senator thinks I am."

"She is a grown woman, sort of. For all her savvy she does the silliest things." Nina shook her head. "One good thing about all this is, I'm sure her daddy is revving up his broom to get her out of here and back under his control."

Scott brightened. "I hadn't thought of that."

"That's why I get the big bucks." She paused, thinking hard. Her phone vibrated. "That's your grandmother. I called her before I called you for an emergency meeting to figure out how to use this. You need to talk to your people. We'll need crowd control. The press will be here to interview Anastasia. Too bad she didn't leave with Carl. We could have been spared the media attention. After my meet with Miss E., I'm going to talk to Anastasia, prep her on what to say." She clicked out of the browser and closed her laptop. She slipped her laptop into its case and swung it over her shoulder. As they walked to the door, she suddenly kissed him and did a little dance. "This is turning out to be a great day."

After her meeting with Miss E., Nina hunted Anastasia down. Anastasia sat by the pool, her dog in her lap, a floppy hat on her head and the smallest white bikini Nina had ever seen, though she had to admit the white looked perfect against Anastasia's almond-colored skin. A bottle of sunblock sat on a table next to her accompanied by a margarita.

A bunch of teens romped in the shallow end of the pool under the watchful gaze of their parents who sunned themselves.

Nina sat down next to Anastasia. "I saw your sex tape."

"Isn't it great?" Anastasia gushed. "I have no idea why you divorced your husband."

Because he was doing this crap while they were married, without the visual proofs. "Let's just say, we drifted apart. Sweetie, I need to know one thing. What were you thinking?" Besides coming up with new ways to embarrass her father. Nina still hadn't answered the senator's frantic calls. She was now up to thirty-one.

Anastasia shrugged. "It seemed like a fun idea at the time."

Nina ground her teeth. "I understand. You were trying to hurt your daddy."

"Daddy only brings me out when it's election time and I have to play the part of the good, dutiful daughter. He doesn't care about me the rest of the time."

"And this is your way of making him notice you."

Anastasia took off her sunglasses. "I don't care anymore."

"What is your mother going to think when she sees it?"

Anastasia put a hand over her mouth, her eyes going wide. "I didn't think of my mother."

"I think you and Carl should date for a while." Nina had thought about ways to avert some of the damage the tape would cause.

"Why should I do that?"

"People have more sympathy for a couple who are dating. Otherwise it just looks like a one-night stand."

"Well, it was. Carl is very nice and I enjoyed my night with him…" Anastasia looked wistful.

Nina had the feeling the date meant more to her than she was letting on. "Then you need to enjoy a little more time with him."

"He did say he thought I'd be perfect for a small part in this new movie he's going to be working on."

"You should be able to leverage this tape into an acting gig." Actresses a lot less skilled than Anastasia had done similar stunts.

A small smile crept across Anastasia face. "I think I'd like to be an actress. I want to have my own life, my own money."

Nina nodded. "I can understand that. The next step is up to Carl. Just talk with him."

"Is he angry with me for leaking the tape?"

"Good God, no," Nina said with a short laugh. "For men, it's a badge of honor that proves their sexual prowess. Carl is thrilled." Not completely the truth. "This is exactly the bump he needed for his career. He's about to direct two episodes for a major TV show…" Her voice trailed off as she stared at Anastasia, suddenly realizing she was the woman Carl needed. She was media savvy, knew how to keep her name in front of the public and Nina herself couldn't ask for a better replacement. "Just call him. I think Carl needs you. You two could get a lot out of this."

Anastasia reached for her phone. "Then I will." She thought for a second. "And then I'll call my mom. At least she'll act like an adult."

"What about your daddy?" Nina repressed a shudder. Dealing with the senator was not going to be pretty.

"I think it's time I dealt with him, too." Anastasia's voice sounded confident, but the look in her eyes held uncertainty. She looked at her watch and tapped the crystal. "Forty-five minutes."

Perplexed, Nina asked. "What do you mean?"

"I calculate he'll be here in about forty-five minutes, so you better get ready for the Parrish temper tantrum." She gave Nina a coy look. "I came by the name legitimately."

"I'd better warn Scott."

Anastasia just nodded. She leaned back against the lounge chair, phone to her ear. Nina stood and headed back into the hotel.

When Anastasia predicted forty-five minutes, she'd been accurate to about thirty-five seconds. Nina warned Scott, but he hadn't needed it. He knew the senator and how his daughter knew which buttons to push.

Senator Richard Parish was a large, bulky man with severe features and angry brown eyes. He stalked into the hotel as though he owned it, followed by his retainers who hustled along in his wake like waves behind a cruise ship.

Scott waited in the lobby, calm and relaxed.

Senator Parrish walked right up to Scott after noticing him and punched at him with his finger. "This is your fault."

Scott didn't back away. With one eyebrow raised, he replied. "I wasn't in the sex tape with your daughter." He couldn't help enjoying the senator's embarrassment.

The elevator doors slid open to reveal Anastasia and Nina. The stepped into the lobby and the senator immediately started to pounce on his daughter.

Before he opened his mouth, Anastasia said sweetly, "Daddy, how nice to see you. Before you say something, do you really want to make a scene in such a public place?"

He clamped his mouth tight over what he'd planned to say.

Anastasia threaded her arm around his. "Let's go upstairs to my suite and talk where it's more private." Her glance included Scott and Nina with a tiny nod of her head.

He stepped into the open elevator followed by Nina and Scott. Scott punched the close-door button before any of the senator's staff could push their way inside.

In her suite, Anastasia sat down in a chair. She looked calm and ready for battle, but Scott saw a slight tremor in her hands.

"Do you really want to have this out in front of people who aren't family?"

"They're my friends." Anastasia's voice was steady, but her eyes showed the beginnings of panic.

Scott stood by the door. Nina sat down opposite Anastasia while her father paced back and forth.

"How could you embarrass me so?"

Anastasia smiled. "Actually, it was pretty easy to do."

"And what about your mother?"

"I talked to Mom and told I was sorry if I hurt her. She's okay with it."

Scott had the feeling the ex-Mrs. Parrish understood exactly why Anastasia had done what she'd done.

"Do you know what kind of damage this is going to do to my campaign?"

"Do you know what kind of damage it's going to do to my acting career?" Anastasia countered. "Nothing."

"Acting career!" the senator thundered. His brown skin went gray as color leeched from his face.

Scott glanced at Nina and mouthed the word *acting*. She nodded slightly and mouthed back, *later*.

"Do you think you can act?"

"I've been acting all my life." Anastasia's face was set with determination.

The senator turned on Scott. "Why didn't you stop her?"

Scott grinned. He was enjoying this way too much. "Number one, I wasn't there. Number two, not my job. Number three, she's a grown woman."

The senator whirled around to glare at Nina. "Why didn't you stop her?"

Nina shrugged. "Not my job, either?" Nina smiled, but

Scott could tell she was trying not to laugh. Hell, he was trying not to laugh.

"You're the big media guru." The senator rubbed his face in frustration. "How do I spin this?"

"Number one, I'm not on your payroll. Number two, I'm not on your payroll. Number three, I'm not on your payroll."

The senator looked like he was going to blow a fuse. "How much? How much would it take for you to repair this…this intolerable situation?"

Nina pursed her lips as though thinking. "You don't have enough money to pay me. Besides, I'm busy and I don't want to work for you."

Scott grinned. The poor senator was having one hellacious day. No one was giving him any love. This man had no problem messing with other people's lives, but his own daughter had just thrown a monkey wrench into his future political plans. All his political maneuverings were designed to someday get him into the White House or as close to it as he could get, and his daughter had scuttled him. Life was good.

The senator tried to say something, but sputtered instead. He shook his head and sputtered some more.

Anastasia stood. "Now, if you'll excuse me, I need to pack. I have to catch the three o'clock plane to LA for my guest-starring role in *Sunset Cop*." She headed for her bedroom and opened the door. Her little dog barked once and leaped at her. She leaned over to pick him up and closed the door behind her.

The senator was still spewing out inarticulate sounds of fury. Nina looked amused and Scott almost felt sorry for him. Senator Parrish's world was one of political backstabbing. He'd never been thwarted before. He might wear expensive suits and handmade shoes, but nothing had prepared this man for his only child's rebellion. This was virgin territory for the senator.

Scott wanted to see how he would handle it. He leaned against the wall and watched the senator continue to pace until he stopped in front of Nina.

"Do something," he demanded. "Help me."

"I'm going to give you the best piece of advice for this situation. Whether you take it or not, I don't care and I won't even bill you for it."

"What?"

"When you talk to the press, you look them straight in the eye and say, *so what*. This is your daughter. Do you want what's best for Anastasia or what's best for yourself?"

"My daughter is not going to be an actress. She is not going to flaunt herself to public."

"News flash," Nina said with a laugh. "Already done and got the T-shirt."

He glared so angrily at Nina that Scott thought his eyes would bug out. Senator Parrish then turned and stormed out of the suite.

"You can lead a senator to reality, but…" Nina shrugged. In the next second, she started to laugh, doubling over.

Scott joined her, the sound echoing off the walls.

The door to the bedroom crept open. "Is he gone?" Anastasia said with a fearful look around the living area.

In between guffaws, Nina said, "He got on his broom… and took…his flying monkeys…home."

Anastasia stepped out of the bedroom. She shook so hard Scott grabbed her and helped her to a chair.

"I wish…" she said.

"Anastasia," Nina said coming to kneel in front of her. "You defied him and now go out there and live your life."

"I talked to Carl and he's okay with the publicity dating," she said, "and I think I'm going to have a publicity baby, too."

"Sweetie," Nina said seriously. "A baby is not an accessory. Just stick with the sex tape."

"Okay," Anastasia said. "I need to finish packing. Thank you for your support. Can I call you if I need advice?"

"You can, but you'll be fine." Nina grabbed Scott's hand and drew him to door. "Bye, see you on TV. And no more sex tapes."

Scott opened the door and they stood in the hall for a moment. "A marriage made in TMZ heaven."

"What do you mean?" He led the way to the elevator. He needed to get back to work.

Nina sighed. "My prediction. Anastasia and Carl are going to really hit it off, get married and end up ruling Hollywood and I'll be knitting baby booties for them within a year. Carl will be thrilled no end."

Scott laughed. "You enjoyed all that, didn't you?"

She twirled around and grabbed him around the shoulders. "I know it's bad, but that is why my job is so much fun." She kissed him.

Scott gripped her tightly and kissed her back. Kissing was a lot of fun, too.

Nina straightened Scott's tie. He enjoyed having her fuss over him. In the last few weeks, he had looked forward to each night he could manage with her, the feel of her body next to his, and the way she looked at him with her sleep-filled eyes in the mornings.

"It's just a press conference," he said as she brushed lint off the sleeve of his jacket.

"This is the first major press conference the hotel is

doing since the change of ownership. You have to set the tone for how the hotel is viewed by the outside world."

"I know how to act professionally."

Nina clicked her tongue. "The press is looking for salacious details in order to make us look stupid. The press needs to fill inches in their newspapers and sound bites on the TV news. They want to see how far they can push you, because prostitution, in their minds, is a victimless crime. You did something most hotels turn a blind eye to."

Scott closed his eyes and counted to ten. The police had conducted a very successful sting operation arresting two bartenders and several waitresses who worked as hookers on the side. Other hotels may turn a blind eye, but he couldn't.

"Can't we just skip the conference and have an early lunch?" He winked at her and she chuckled.

"Go out there and do your grandmother proud. Don't forget the chief of police's name is Luis Mendoza and the DA's name is Porter Atwell. This was a major operation for them, so make nice. And you'll have two new friends."

Scott shrugged. The press conference was being held in a conference room on the second floor. Already the press had dragged in all their equipment. Cables crisscrossed the corridor and made walking a nightmare. Several news reporters were already talking to the cameras setting up the intro to what was happening.

"You know the questions they're going to ask," Nina continued, "and you have your answers. If they ask something you don't want to answer just say you can't comment on that now." After one last tug of his tie, Nina pushed him toward the podium and the other men waiting there. "Have fun with this." She withdrew to stand to the side out of the cameras' viewing field.

Luis Mendoza wore his full dress uniform and looked

official. He was a tall man with a military-straight bearing, black hair going silver at the temples and cool blue eyes. Porter Atwell was smaller and slim. He wore a dark blue power suit and looked ready to take on the world. He greeted Scott with a handshake.

"Ready for this?" Porter Atwell asked with a nod at the restless reporters.

"I don't much care for press conferences. Reporters never get the facts straight no matter how many times you correct them."

Atwell nodded. "They're just looking for the sensational."

"I lived in DC for three years and it wasn't any different there," Scott said. Actually, it was probably worse. Reporters salivated over the most minor misdoings of anyone in government.

Chief of Police Mendoza stood in front of the row of microphones arranged across the front edge of the podium where he spoke about the sting operation and how it had been conducted. He then turned the mics over to Atwell who spoke briefly about how the laws of the city had been upheld. Finally, it was Scott's turn.

"Mr. Russell," a woman shouted at him. She was sleek and polished-looking in a gray suit and purple scarf loosely draped about her neck. "Don't you worry that people aren't going to want to stay in this hotel because they can't have 'fun' considering the heightened security?" She punctuated the word fun with clawlike fingers.

"Having fun isn't against the law. Breaking the law isn't having fun. Especially when you get caught."

"But Mr. Russell," the woman pushed, "this is the price of doing business in a city like Reno."

"Things change and as a law-abiding citizen I'm sure

you understand that the laws apply to everyone." Maybe not as equally as they should, but the law was the law.

"But these situations always happen here."

"Tradition isn't necessarily a good thing." Scott caught sight of Nina nodding in agreement. She smiled encouragingly at him. "Robberies happen, people are conned. Those are traditions we'd like to get rid of. Correct?"

The woman nodded.

"You run a clean house or you don't. There's no gray area in between. Casa de Mariposa wants to be a hotel where the safety and protection of guests is paramount. As director of security here, I've put into place a number of new programs designed to keep this hotel as safe as I can make it."

"Does that include increased security around that ten-million-dollar jackpot guests can view in the casino?" a man at the back of the room shouted.

"Of course." Scott didn't want to go into that headache, but he had to admit the casino had been hopping with tons of new business simply because people wanted to see what ten million dollars looked like. And with each million shrink-wrapped to the size of a box large enough to hold a dozen bottles of wine, people couldn't help crowding around to dream about winning it.

"We invite you to take a tour of the casino," Scott continued, "and check out the increased security for yourselves." *Just don't drool on the glass casing.*

Chief Mendoza stepped up. "Thank you all for coming today. Any more questions can be directed to my office. You all know how to get ahold of one of my assistants." He efficiently shut the conference down.

Nina curled a hand around Scott's. "Not bad."

"A part of me thinks you felt I couldn't make a sentence."

"You get so scowly-faced sometimes and people stop talking."

"That never works with you."

"I've dealt with temperamental tween stars. They're great training ground for anything." Nina and Scott walked out of the conference room, staying away from the news people who looked like they had more questions.

"Now I have to deal with another situation." Gary White had become a real thorn in his side.

"Are you going to give him a stern talking-to? Can I watch?"

"You sound a little too excited."

"I'm just trying to be a part of your world."

"You're a scary woman, Nina."

She smiled smugly. "I know. But in a fun way."

He shook his head as he headed back toward the security control center. She kissed him. "I'll meet you for lunch. I make a mean meat loaf sandwich."

Two detectives waited for him in his office.

"Detective Logan," Scott said. "I assume you're ready." They had one more arrest to make.

Logan nodded. Scott opened the door between his office and the control center. Gary White sat at the monitors looking bored.

"Gary," Scott said. "My office."

Gary glared at Scott, but stood and walked in. He stopped when he saw the detectives.

"Sit down, Gary. This is Detective Logan and Detective Greene. They have some questions for you."

"About what?" Gary looked relaxed yet wary.

Detective Logan smiled. "I believe you know a bartender named Bart Olsen."

Gary nodded. "He works the night shift in the casino bar."

"Mr. Olsen has been telling quite a story and you're the lead character."

"I hardly know the guy," Gary sputtered. "I see him in the halls and say hi, but that's pretty much all."

"I think you know him better than that. We've been looking into your finances. You seem to have a lot of stuff for someone who makes a relatively modest salary."

Gary shrugged. "I'm a good saver. My wife works."

"Enough to afford a Corvette, a Harley, an RV, a Jet Ski and a number of other little luxuries. You have a sweet little hideaway in Tahoe…"

"Great for family getaways," Gary replied.

He continued to look relaxed, but Scott noticed his hands stiffened.

"You paid cash for your little getaway. Nobody has that kind of money just lying around doing nothing."

Gary frowned. "I said I'm a good saver."

Detective Logan crowded him. "All in all, Gary, we just think you're guilty of taking a little on the side. We don't think you're the mastermind. If you have anything you want to say, say it now and we'll talk to the judge for you. Get you a light sentence."

Gary laughed harshly. "I know my rights. I want a lawyer."

"We can't do anything for you then."

Gary's face went hard. "I want a lawyer."

"Okay then." Logan pushed himself to his feet and smiled benevolently at Gary. "Gary White, you're under arrest. We have a long, long list of charges." The detective rattled off the Miranda warning while he cuffed Gary.

Scott had been wanting to say this for weeks, but couldn't until the detectives completed their investigation. "And I'd like to add, you're fired. I'm going to get lunch now."

Gary grinned. "I'll be out in a couple hours, boss. Have my final paycheck ready for me. I'll be picking it up."

"You do that," Scott said.

Detective Logan grasped Gary by the arm and pushed him out the door. "On behalf of the Reno police department, thank you for cooperation, Mr. Russell."

"Anytime," Scott replied. "Anytime."

Scott felt good. He could cross another item off his to-do list. He closed his office door and headed for the elevators and Nina.

Chapter 11

The music was loud and infectious. Scott's foot tapped to the beat. He sat in a booth, a bowl of pretzels in front of him and a Long Island Iced Tea that he'd barely touched. Nina bounced around the dance floor teaching Miss E. the samba, her hips swaying back and forth as she twisted and turned. Miss E. tried to copy the movement, but her seventy-eight year old body wasn't as agile.

Nina looked particularly alluring in a little black dress that set off the slope of her shoulders and revealed her long, shapely legs. She'd pulled her hair severely back from her face and secured a bright red spray of flowers behind one ear. He waited patiently for his turn on the dance floor with her.

Her parents partnered with Lydia and Maya while Kenzie taught Jasper. Hotel guests circled the dance floor watching; a few stood a bit away, following the steps by watching the other dancers.

"Congrats, bro," Hunter said as he slid into the booth to sit across from Scott. "I heard you and the police broke up the bookie ring working here in the casino."

"Yeah, and I'm down another four security people." Not that the security guards were implicated in the illegal bookie ring. They'd known all about it and done nothing, nor had they apprised Scott of what was going on, because they didn't want to completely endanger their little cut-backs. Scott was deeply concerned about the widespread corruption in his security personnel. "I've been contacting as many of my old army buddies as I can find and having them come in for interviews." At least, he'd have people around he trusted.

"Who knew all this was going right under Jasper's nose."

Scott shook his head. "Jasper's not a bad guy, but he is all about having fun. And Louisa was no help. Do you think she knew what was going on?"

"I think she was more interested in making money than understanding how crime could work its way into a solid operation like this hotel."

"I talked to some of the other security directors at other hotels," Scott said, "and they seem to have the idea this is just the cost of doing business no matter how much they dislike it." Scott didn't understand it. "I know the cost of doing business can be compromised for good reasons. I got enough of that in the army where the big picture mentality is more important than the details." Miss E. was the least tolerant of crime in the casino. She wanted a squeaky clean, crime-free business. Scott doubted she'd have a one hundred percent crime-free casino, but he could come close.

"Has any more counterfeit money shown up?" Hunter asked.

"The classes from the Secret Service have really helped. Knowing that our people are well trained means the criminals are staying clear of here. I've had other hotels call to ask how we're doing and I keep telling them to talk to the Secret Service. But it's like Whac-A-Mole. I keep hitting the mole, but another one pops up someplace else." Even the new design of the hundred-dollar bills hadn't kept counterfeiters from copying it. And every time he found a new way to spot the fake bills, the people passing them found new ways to get around his protocols.

His gaze followed Nina as she swayed to the music. What had started out as a friendly rivalry with her had changed to something deeper, more meaningful. He didn't just like having sex with her. He liked hanging out with her. He liked just everything about her.

"Do you want to marry her?" Hunter asked.

"Do you think you'd just take a moment to lead in to the question gradually? Beat around the bush a bit."

Hunter laughed. "I'm your brother. I don't have to beat around the bush. I get to ask questions outright. And you have to answer."

"No, I don't." Scott glared at his brother.

"Don't make me put you in a headlock and give you a noogie," Hunter warned.

"I would like to see you try. Army ranger here." Scott pointed at his chest.

"I don't want to embarrass you in front of your girl."

Scott wondered what would happen if they started wrestling right here in the bar in front of guests and family.

Nina whirled and grabbed a bystander and drew him out on the floor.

"Really."

"If I reach over and give you a good, little tap, you'll get some sympathy from your girl."

Scott glared at Hunter. "I don't think so."

"Just a little tap." Hunter burst out laughing. "What's really going on with you and Nina?"

"Other than having a good time, I don't know." Scott wanted more, but did Nina?

"Don't you want to know?"

"She's good at her job. She's in high demand and I know

she's fielded four or five new offers." Of which one was in Milan.

Hunter burst out into laughter again. "Do you hear yourself?"

Scott eyed him. "What do you mean?"

"This, my brother, is what is called karma. You've used the same excuse for years to avoid a relationship. Your job moves you around too much. It's dangerous. You're in high demand."

Scott fingered the dish of pretzels. "I know you're my brother and all, but feel free not to be so honest with me."

Hunter grinned. "What fun would that be? At least Donovan isn't here to enjoy your misery."

Donovan was finally on his way. He'd be in Reno in a week, just in time to launch the holiday menus he'd been working on with Manny Torres. Christmas and New Year's Day were never going to be just roast turkey again. And in a couple weeks, Nina would probably be heading out to her next job. One of the offers was to start the week after New Year's.

Scott still had so much to do. And Nina, too. Sometimes he didn't think she slept. She was always bubbling with new ideas to promote everything. And now that the spa was almost ready to open, she'd managed to get the mayor of Reno to attend as well as a jazz band.

"You love her. I can tell," Hunter said.

Scott shook his head. "I don't know. I like her a lot." Did he love her? He wasn't certain. Though he remembered a conversation he'd had with his grandmother a long time ago. His first love had been in high school. The lead cheerleader for the football team had been cute and bubbly. Scott was the popular quarterback who had been the object of her interest. He'd told Miss E. he was in love with her, but she had asked if he liked her. Scott had thought long and hard about it and realized he didn't like her. She was more interested in dating popular guys and wearing designer clothes, than being likable. Miss E. had told Scott that he had to like someone first before he could fall in love. Funny, he couldn't remember the cheerleader's name.

Was he in love with Nina? Part of him said yes and another part said not yet. But the right conditions were there to be in love.

"Stop lying to yourself, Scott."

He frowned. "What do you mean?"

"I can see it on your face. You're trying to talk yourself out of loving Nina, but it's too late."

"You don't know anything." Being on the offensive with his brother was not a good place to be.

"You talk about her all the time. You can't stop watching her. And on a number of occasions, you chose her over your job. You love her."

"I doubt she's going to be around once the New Year's Eve party and your wedding are over." Scott felt uncomfortable under his brother's scrutiny.

"You're never going to find out unless you ask her." Hunter shoved himself out of the booth and walked to Lydia, falling into step with her.

Scott didn't know what to say to Nina. He'd never been in love before. Darn! He'd just admitted it to himself. What was he going to do? He didn't know, and the longer he watched Nina as she twisted around the dance floor the more he wanted to grab her and run off with her.

Nina grinned at him and suddenly darted across the floor to grab his hand and pull him after her, her hips twisting in tune with the music. The samba had a sensual, hypnotic beat. Desire for Nina flooded him. What he really wanted to do was fling her over his shoulder and take her to his suite and spend the rest of the night showing her how much he adored her.

He loved her.

Nina stood in front the huge whiteboard she'd set up in her suite. Rows and columns were spread across it and each event she'd planned over the next few weeks was written in the corresponding box.

"Let's talk security," Nina said over her shoulder to Scott.

Scott stood behind her studying the schedule. "I've filled all the empty positions and added ten extra guards to work the casino."

Nina glanced at the dining table. "Have you chosen which photos you want to exhibit in the show?"

"I'm having a hard time coming up with something that will look good with all those professional photos you've managed to grab for the show."

"The professionals are the draw," she replied. "You're not competing with them, you're a supporting player along with the other artists Caroline got." Caroline Fairchild had turned out to be a treasure. Nina had tried to get the exhibit together for Veteran's Day, but that hadn't worked out. Caroline had suggested she take over and had postponed the photo exhibit until Christmas.

Caroline was organized, methodical and thorough. She'd contacted the artists, photographers and sculptors.

Nina thought having the exhibit spread out through the lobby and corridors leading to the casino would be good exposure, but Scott vetoed the idea, insisting the exhibit be in one place that was easy to secure. They'd decided on the spa lobby for its grand opening the week before Christmas. Most of the exhibit was in already in place. Caroline was just waiting on Scott and a couple other photographers.

"I don't feel qualified," Scott said. He shuffled through his photographs.

"Are you kidding? You're an artist."

"So are you. You should put some of your booties on display."

Nina kissed him on the cheek. "You are sweet. I'm already in the bootie hall of fame."

He chuckled. "I've chosen the ones I want to show. I'll have them framed and sent over to Caroline by Friday."

"Thank you."

He wrapped an arm around her and pulled her close. His kiss was warm and lingering and Nina leaned into it.

"No smoochies," she said though she didn't mean it. "We have work to do. You are now part of this community and Reno is your home. So get those photos over to the framer."

He kissed her again. She closed her eyes. Desire flooded through her. She didn't know what she was going to do. She'd had several job offers and had been surprised at herself for being uninterested. Being near Scott had taken precedence over her career and she was both fascinated and saddened by her response. She spent long hours puzzling over what she wanted. She knew she wanted to be with Scott, but at the same time she wanted her career.

"I said no smoochies." She pushed him away. "Don't you have a meeting scheduled?"

He glanced at his watch and frowned. "I almost forgot." He kissed her again, his kiss filled with promise. "Dinner tonight?"

"My place? How about eight o'clock?" Her schedule was so filled that she sometimes forgot to eat.

"Don't forget." He grinned as he closed the door behind him.

Nina sighed. She needed to talk to her mom.

* * *

Grace arranged a fruit salad on two plates and set them on Nina's dining room table. "I knew you didn't each breakfast or lunch."

Nina sat at the table. The doors to the balcony stood open and a cool breeze swept inside.

"What's wrong?" Grace asked.

"How did you do it?" Nina dug into her salad not realizing she was starving until this moment.

"Do what, dear?" Grace poured water into glasses.

"You have it all, Mom. How did you manage to combine a career, a marriage and motherhood? You make it all look so effortless."

"I had to choose what was most important to me and work everything else around it. Your father made the same decision."

Nina rubbed her temple. "But…"

"We made the decision to be a family," Grace continued. "It wasn't always easy. I turned down a record deal and your dad declined a job with a jazz band. Neither one of us wanted to be away from our family."

"I know you sacrificed a lot for us."

"This is about Scott, isn't it?"

Nina sighed. "I like him. I…I…" The *love* word just wasn't ready to come out.

"You love him." Grace's voice was filled with amusement.

"I like the way he thinks. I like the way he irritates me." She liked the way he made love to her, though that would remain unsaid. Her parents weren't prudes, but Nina still couldn't talk about her sex life with her mother. "I like everything about him even if he's wound a little tight."

"I noticed you kind of unwound him."

"What do I do?"

Grace patted her hand. "What's the problem?"

"I want to be with him, but I want to do my job. I've fielded seven offers in the last two months and none of them were interesting. Even the President of the United States has put out feelers. He wants me to help train his media people, especially with midterm elections coming up. I can't turn down the president, but I have no desire to say yes."

"Honey, I turned down huge rock stars. One I had to pass up because your brother was going through the terrible twos and I couldn't leave him. And I'd just found out I was pregnant with you. You have to figure out what is important to you and once you know, you make a decision based on that."

"You make it sound so easy."

"It's not." Grace smiled. "But you make a decision and live with it. That's the rule."

What decision did she want to make? "I don't want another failure like Carl. I put his welfare above my own. I made all the compromises and he didn't." In part, she was as much at fault as he was, no matter how much blame she heaped on him. "I didn't insist he put as much effort into our marriage as I did."

"Your marriage with Carl was just another media job. You just didn't know that until too late. Scott doesn't need you to do your job for him. He has nothing he wants, except maybe you." Her mother took her hand. "You need to talk to Scott. You need to know how he feels. And you need to tell him how you feel. Life is all about compromise."

Nina spent the afternoon getting ready for her dinner with Scott. She allowed her father to make the dinner while she nervously fussed over what she should wear, how she should look. Never had something that seemed so simple felt so complicated.

Scott knocked on her door exactly at eight o'clock. Kong barked once and wagged his tail in anticipation. Scott had come to enjoy Kong and the little dog was Scott's new best friend.

She smoothed her favorite Vivienne Westwood dress over her hips. She loved the grayish-green silk with ruching down the side seams adding to her curves. She opened the door and his eyes went wide at the sight of her even though everything was covered from the high neck to the long sleeves.

"I brought flowers." He handed her a small bouquet. "And wine." He held up a bottle of pinot grigio and a squeaky toy for Kong who accepted it politely and immediately began to play with it.

"Thank you." The fragrance of the flowers swirled over her. Nervously, she walked back to the kitchen to find a vase and put the flowers in it. She set the flowers on the table between the flickering candles.

"Something smells good." He sniffed experimentally.

"My father made Brazilian chicken. You'll like it."

He opened the wine and poured it into wineglasses. "So what's the occasion?"

"I needed to talk something over with you." Did he detect the tiniest quiver in her voice? She hoped not.

His eyebrows rose. "Must be important."

They sat down at the table and she uncovered the chicken breasts covered in her father's special sauce and resting on a bed of rice. Another dish contained perfectly braised asparagus.

She sipped her wine nervously. He served himself and then her. "My job is coming to an end here. I've been fielding several offers and having a hard time deciding what to do next."

His face went still and quiet. "What kind of job offers?"

Nervously, she plucked at her napkin. "The President of the United States is one."

"And that would entail what?"

"Moving to Washington, DC for a few months and working with his media department and coming up with a media campaign for the midterm elections."

He sighed. "That's an incredible offer."

"And a hard one to turn down."

"Maybe you shouldn't turn it down."

Her heart sank. "I don't know. DC..." She grimaced.

"What else?"

"A couple movies, a has-been actor trying to make a comeback, Fashion Week in Milan where I'd have to start now." She took a bite of her chicken, but the food seemed to stick in her throat. She took a sip of water to wash it down, then set her fork down, uncertain she could continue. "I'm not sure where I want to go. I don't know what I want." How had she gone from being so self-assured to this conflicting set of emotions?

"Sounds like you have a decision to make."

"What would you do if you were in my shoes?"

He took her hand. "Nina, I don't want you to go."

She stared at him. She didn't think he'd say anything. They'd had a lot of fun, more than she'd ever had with any other man. "What are you saying?"

He rubbed her fingers with his thumb. "Stay with me. Stay here in Reno."

"Why?"

"I've never said this before to a woman, so I'm not sure I'm going to say the right words."

"Get it out?"

"I like you a lot. I've come to care for you. We've been having a good time and I want to keep exploring it. But

I don't want to stand in the way of your career. You have an incredible opportunity in front of you. I don't want to be Carl."

She took a deep sip of her wine.

Scott's phone chirped. He looked surprised while he dug it out of his pocket. "It's Belle."

"You better answer it. She would never call you at this time of night if it wasn't important."

He answered and listened for a moment. "I'll be right down. Call the police, tell them what's going on." He disconnected, shoved back from the table and stood.

"Scott."

"Armed men are in the casino." He ran out the door.

Nina followed him to the elevator, chilled with fear. "They have guns and anyone who knows our routine might chance a payoff of ten million dollars. They didn't come for the buffet." He jabbed at the elevator button. The doors slid open and he stepped inside.

"Where do you think you're going?" Scott demanded as she stepped in beside him

"You deal with the problem, I'll deal with the media."

The elevator descended. The doors opened at the second floor. Scott left and before he'd a gone a few feet, Nina jabbed for the first floor. She wondered why he'd gotten off, but didn't think anything else. As the doors closed, he turned, panic on his face and shouted, "No." He ran back toward the elevator, but the doors closed.

Nina frowned. What was wrong with Scott? She said she'd take care of the media who would probably already be congregating outside the front doors.

The elevator came to a stop and the doors slid open and she found herself with two very large guns pointing directly at her.

Chapter 12

Nina sat on the hard floor of the casino, legs crossed, trying to be comfortable and not think about the fear clouding her thinking. Miss E. sat next to her looking more than just disgruntled. She glanced around trying to get a head count. She estimated about fifty casino guests sat on the floor. How odd to see the casino almost empty. She had to assume the moment the gang of thieves started brandishing their guns, people had run for the doors.

A woman behind Nina sobbed. Nina turned and tried for an encouraging smile, but her lips quivered. "It's going to be all right."

The woman, heavily pregnant, tried to smile through the tears blotting her face, but her lips didn't move. She held the hand of a man who hovered over her as though trying to hide her.

Nina tried to keep people calm, but they were all frightened. Now she knew why Scott had gotten off on the second floor even though the control room was on the first and tried to stop her from continuing down to the lobby.

She counted ten men, all dressed in black with black masks to hide their faces, along with some very big guns. She had no idea what kind of guns they were, but they looked lethal. She assumed they were assault weapons of some sort with lots of bullets.

Two of the armed, masked men tapped at the Lucite enclosure holding the ten million dollars. Nina knew they weren't going to break into the box. The Lucite was three inches thick. Two more men were robbing the casino guests of cash, valuables and cell phones.

An elderly woman sat on the other side of Nina, clutching her purse to her. When one of them grabbed the purse and turned it over to scatter the contents on the floor, the woman gasped. She wore a lovely set of pearls, a wide gold wedding band and a nice watch. The robber grabbed her arm to twist off the watch.

"Gimme the ring," he snarled.

"She can't," Nina said.

"I won't," the woman said, clutching her hand to her chest. "I've worn this for sixty years, young man, and I'm not taking it off."

"She has arthritis, she won't be able to get it over the knuckle," Nina explained.

He growled deep in his throat after tossing the woman's cell phone in a sack along with the watch and the pearls. He rifled through her wallet and drew out all the money he found and dropped it in the sack. He left the ring and stood in front of Nina.

Nina watched him carefully. He was dressed in black. He had a small eagle tattoo on the back of his hand and wore a teardrop diamond earring in one ear. The diamond was fake.

"Earrings," he said.

Darn, she thought. "You can't have my earrings. They were a gift." Besides they were real diamonds.

"Do I look like I care?"

She leaned toward him. "From Angelina Jolie."

His eyes narrowed. "I know who you are."

She took the earrings off. She knew this man. Gary

White had the same eagle tattoo on the back of his hand. Having identified him she saw all the other similarities that told her who he was. Her gaze swept over the other robbers. She had the feeling they were all security guards dismissed by Scott. She handed him the earrings.

"Bracelet." He gestured at the glittering cuff she wore. She twisted the cuff off and handed it to him.

"Phone."

"I was eating dinner in my room and didn't think to grab my purse. I don't have my phone." Which was in her pocket, but she wasn't about to tell him that. She pasted the most innocent expression on her face that she could. In the distance she heard sirens. "The police are here."

He ignored her and moved to Miss E. without comment, Miss E. handed over her phone and her watch. He passed down the line. Nina watched him, scooting back carefully into the group of hostages behind her so neither he nor his cohorts could see her. She eased her phone out of her pocket and placed it low in her lap. She texted to Scott,

Gary White holding 55 hostages with me and Miss E.

She rapidly went through her settings and set her phone to silence, even disabling the vibrate setting. She didn't want the tiniest sound to alert Gary that she still had her phone. She thrust the phone under her thigh to hide it.

Several of the men stood in front of the ten-million-dollar jackpot, drilling into the three-inch-thick Lucite. On the floor at their feet was an electric saw. Nina watched, knowing they weren't going to get inside easily. Another man assembled a number of banker's boxes. Each shrink-wrapped million would just fit inside one box.

Miss E. looked calm and serene as she told people to cooperate with the robbers.

Nina had to do something. She glanced down at her phone. Scott had sent a text.

Tell them you'll give them the key to the display in return for letting hostages go.

Nina glanced around and saw Gary sitting on a stool in front of a slot machine. He fingered his gun, his gaze on Miss E. Nina tried to get his attention. She thrust her hand in the air and gestured at him.

Gary slid off the stool and approached her.

She pointed at the Lucite box. "I can save you some time getting into the case. I can get you the key."

"How?" He leaned over her trying to intimidate her.

"Let the hostages go first."

His eyebrows rose. "Then I have no leverage."

"I'll stay," Nina offered.

He eyed her thoughtfully for a few seconds, then turned and walked over to the knot of men next to the display case. Nina thought she heard comments of assent. Two men nodded.

"It doesn't look like the robbery is going quite the way Gary thought it would," Miss E. said with a wry chuckle.

"You recognized him, too."

"The tattoo on the back of his hand is a dead giveaway."

"That's why I recognized him, too."

"That's why I keep my tattoo hidden." Miss E. grinned.

"You have a tattoo?" The thought of Miss E. having a tattoo struck her as too funny. "I'll giggle about this when we're no longer hostages. And I'm going to want to see it."

"Not a chance. Trust me, you don't want to see them. When I was thirty they were butterflies and now that I'm seventy-eight they're condors."

The image captured her imagination. "Don't make me laugh. This is not the time."

Miss E. chuckled again.

Gary walked back to Nina. "Get the key. We're not letting the hostages go until I see you with it in your hand."

"Sure." Nina pushed to her feet.

Gary stared at the floor and then backhanded her. "I said no phones."

Nina's head flew back. Anger grew in her. "So, I lied."

He glared at her as he escorted her to the casino entrance.

Nina rubbed her cheek. She was going to have a bruise shortly.

The lobby was completely empty. Outside the front doors, Nina could see police vehicles and SWAT trucks in the street with armed police officers watching the front doors.

Gary shoved her toward the administrative door. "Get that key."

"I will." Nina strode confidently to the door leading into the administration area and Scott's control center.

The control room was eerily quiet and tense. The newest hires sat with their training officers. They'd been learning the routines of the casino and how to spot criminal activity. Scott stood in the center, working hard to keep his fear for Nina and his grandmother under control. He couldn't afford to give in to his fear as he watched Nina talk to Gary White. Seeing her in such danger made him want to rip out a wall. He hated feeling helpless watching the woman he loved being manhandled.

Scott watched Gary White shove Nina. She managed to keep on her feet, but his anger rose, supplanting his fear.

Gary White had no idea what was going to happen to him once Scott got ahold of him.

"He took the bait," Belle Sampson said. She sat at the computer, eyes glued to the monitor. "What are we going to do now? Just give it to him?"

Chief of Police Luis Mendoza stood with Scott along with the head of the SWAT team. "We'll not only give him the key, but encourage him to leave."

Scott couldn't keep the grin off his face. "We're going to let him and his little gang walk out the door with all that counterfeit money."

Belle twisted to look at him and Chief Mendoza. "What did you just say?"

"All those bundles are counterfeit cash I borrowed from the Secret Service. There are real bills on top to make it look right, but underneath each one of those bills is stamped Counterfeit."

"But what happens if Gary finds out?"

"Do you really think he's going to sit there and unwrap every bundle? He's going to wait until he's somewhere safe." Scott was pretty pleased with himself at scoring the counterfeit money. Sweet-talking the Secret Service into letting him borrow it had been the highlight of his week. He hadn't been too happy placing real money in the display case, though he understood the need to show what ten million looked like.

"So you're going to let him walk out of here?"

"We're going to pretend to try and stop him," Luis Mendoza said, "but every bundle has a little GPS in the middle that will allow us to track it. And once they're free of the casino, we'll grab them."

Belle turned back to the monitor. "You were expecting this, weren't you?"

Scott shook his head. "I like to be prepared. The min-

ute Gary made bail, I had a feeling that wouldn't go away.
I was expecting something, just not sure what."

Belle grinned. "Nina is on her way."

"I'll meet her and bring her back here." Scott left the
control room grateful for just a few moments alone with
her.

He caught Nina as she half ran down the hall. "It's Gary
White and I think all the other men with him are some of
the people you let go."

"We figured this out even before you texted me." He
grabbed her and kissed her hard enough to make her gasp.

Her arms snaked around him. "I'm scared."

"Everything is going to work out. You're doing great."
He hugged her tightly and kissed the tender spot on her
cheek before opening the door of the control room. "Nina,
this is Chief Luis Mendoza of the Reno PD and that's Max
Burning Bear, head of SWAT."

Nina nodded at the two men. "How is this going to
work?"

"Here's the key to the display case." Scott handed her a
long tube. "It inserts into a hole at the bottom of the case
facing the bar. The rod acts as a sensor that deactivates
the signal that keeps the door locked. Once the signal is
deactivated the door will swing open."

Scott could see the fear in her eyes. He wanted to hold
her and murmur encouraging words into her ear, but he
knew time was short. He needed to get Gary and his people to let the hostages go and get them out of the casino.
He hated sending Nina back.

"But first," Chief Mendoza said, "Mr. Russell will es-
cort you back to the casino. He'll get the hostages out. Do
not hand the key over until the hostages are safe outside."

"Are you going to just let them leave?" Nina asked.

"We're not going to do anything to stop them," Scott

replied. "My priority is keeping the guests safe." And you and my grandmother.

"But all that money…"

"It's counterfeit, Miss Torres," Chief Mendoza said quietly. "And they won't get far. Each bundle has a tracking device embedded in it."

"Oh." Nina's eyes grew wide and she laughed. "Miss E. knows it's counterfeit. That's why she isn't putting up any fight."

"Exactly." Scott hugged her again. "So let's get back to the casino."

They left the control room. Scott could feel Nina trembling with anxiety.

"Don't think about it," Scott told her quietly as they paused in front of the door leading to the lobby. He pulled her into his arms and kissed her. "I'm right next to you."

"Shouldn't you have a gun?" she asked.

"Not at the moment. A gun will just escalate the danger." He put a hand on the doorknob and twisted it. Before he opened the door he gave her one last kiss and murmured, "I love you."

"What?"

"I love you."

"You're telling me this now!" She stared at him in confusion.

"Do you know a better time?"

"Yes, and this isn't it." She gestured at the door and he opened it. Nina stepped into the lobby and he heard her breath catch in her throat as she walked determinedly toward the two gunmen at the entrance to the casino, their lethal-looking weapons pointed directly at her. Pride filled Scott for a moment as she held up the key.

"Let everyone go," she said.

* * *

The hostages filed out one by one. Gary kept his rifle pointed at Scott and Nina. "I want a guarantee of safe passage."

"You got it," Scott said.

Gary frowned. "You're making this too easy."

"The money's insured," Scott replied. "Rule number one, my responsibility is to end this as quick and safely as possible. I want you out of this casino. I want you out of this city."

Gary's frown relaxed. The men around the display case were loading each shrink-wrapped package into the banker's boxes. One man wheeled a hand dolly up to the boxes and started loading them.

The last hostage was Miss E. Gary stopped her. "Not you."

"All the hostages."

"I'm changing the plan, Russell," Gary growled. He grabbed Nina, his assault rifle pointed at Scott. "Get out of here. I'll let them go once the vans are loaded. If I see one cop, I'll kill this one first." He jerked Nina forward.

"No." Scott started to argue.

"You have no say in the matter."

The man with the dolly started wheeling it out the back of the casino, around the pool to the adjacent parking lot. Several other men carried the boxes that didn't fit on the dolly. They also departed out the back door.

Nina and Miss E. were herded along at the rear.

Scott watched helplessly. "If you harm them…"

White just laughed.

"I'll be fine," Nina called. "I won't let anything happen to Miss E."

Gary shoved her and she stumbled, catching the edge

of a slot machine and righting herself. She tried to keep a brave look on her face, but Scott could see the fear in her eyes.

"If you so much as hurt one hair on their heads, I will hunt you down to the ends of the earth and you will take a long time to die."

"I'm not afraid of you," Gary said, bravado in his tone.

"That's your second mistake today," Scott said quietly. The rage he felt every time Gary touched Nina grew stronger.

Gary scoffed and turned on his heel toward the back doors of the casino.

Nina held Miss E.'s hand while Gary herded them toward the van. A second van was parked next to it. Full darkness had descended and the lights of Reno shone bright in the distance. Nina could hear the sound of a helicopter overhead.

Once there, Gary waved the big rifle in her face. "Get in the van."

"You said you'd let us go." He grabbed her arm. Nina struggled, but he held her too tightly.

Gary smiled. "I lied."

"I'm not going anywhere with you." She tried to pull away from him, but he grabbed her around the waist and tried to lift her into the van. "Let go." Nina wriggled herself free and stepped back. "You've got what you want, now leave us."

She wasn't going anywhere with him if she could help it. She didn't know if he'd kill her, but if he were angry enough, he might and then she wouldn't see Scott again, or Miss E. or Kenzie, or her family. She needed to tell Scott some very important words. He'd bared his heart to her and she owed him her own words. She loved him and hadn't known until now with the huge gun pointed at her face. Her heart stopped and fear bubbled up inside her. If nothing else, she needed to protect Miss. E.

"Forget them," someone inside the van yelled. "Get in."

"She's coming with us."

A man poked his head out of the side of the van. "Russell will hunt us down if we take his woman. Leave her. Leave the granny, too."

Gary shook his head, determined to get Nina in the van. Nina took another step back. She wasn't going to make it easy for him.

"Get in," the man said in an exasperated tone. Gary raised his gun and hit her hard in the face. She fell to her knees and Miss E. screamed.

"Stop being stupid and leave her." The man reached out, grabbed Gary's shirt, hauled him into the van and shouted, "Go. Go. Go."

The van peeled out of the parking lot, the second one following.

"I know what you were doing," Miss E. commented.

"What was I doing?"

"Being uncooperative, loud and difficult." Miss E. helped her to her feet. She swayed a moment getting her balance.

"Or they could have just shot me." Nina put a hand to her face. Why did he have to hit her?

"That would never have happened. If there is one person Gary is afraid of, it's Scott."

The back doors of the casino burst open and men in black with great big guns poured out, running toward Nina and Miss E., surrounding them.

"Miss E., Ms. Torres," someone said, "let's get you back inside. And safe."

As Nina walked back into the casino, a line of patrol cars followed the vans at a distance. Gary wasn't going to get away. Nina felt immense satisfaction knowing he would get his reward soon.

Nina lay on her sofa, an ice pack on the side of her face. She allowed its coldness to ease the ache. Her mother and father fussed over her.

"I'm fine, Mom," she said.

"You have a black eye, a wrenched shoulder and a bruised wrist."

"Mom, I have five brothers. Trust me, this is nothing." Nina recalled a number of glorious fights with her brothers with them ending up with the ice packs while she'd gloated bruise-free.

"You could have been killed," Grace said, worry adding new lines to her face.

"I wasn't. He had no intention of killing me or Miss E. Gary is nothing but a punk and a bully. In his mind, he was hurting Scott."

Her mother sat down next to her. "But he hurt you and if I'd a gun he'd be dead."

A knock sounded on the door to her suite. Manny opened it to let Scott in. He gestured at Grace who stood. She leaned over and kissed Nina on the forehead. "We'll leave you two alone and check in on you later."

"Thanks, Mom."

Her parents left after asking about Miss E. Scott assured them his grandmother was fine. Jasper was with her and would take good care of her.

"That's a shiner." Scott sat down next to her, looking critically at her eyes.

"I'm kind of proud of it. If Gary hadn't had a gun on me, he'd have suffered worse."

"Then it's a good thing he's now in police custody."

"I was so angry. He ruined my date with you."

Scott kissed her, his lips soft against her. "Ruined my date, too."

She tried to grin, but her mouth hurt a little, too. "Now, about those three little words."

"I said them. I meant them. What else is there to say?"

She studied him with her one eye. "Now is the right time to say them. I'm safe and except for the tenderness in my shoulder, wrist and face, I'm mostly healthy."

"I love you."

Nina gripped his hand and pulled his fingers to her lips. She kissed them. "I love you, too. I didn't know for sure until Gary pointed that great big gun at me and I saw my life spread out in front and the only thing I'd done of any real importance was work. That's not what I want to be."

"No. You're more than you think. You're a great daughter, a great sister and you were a good wife to Carl."

"And look how that worked out for me."

"You and I are going to have a terrific marriage."

She stared at him, her mouth open. "Are you asking me to marry you?"

"Isn't that what I just said?"

"You smooth-talking romantic."

"I love you, Nina."

"If my face and body didn't hurt so much, I'd show you how much I love you, but I think I need more ice packs." She paused and grinned slightly at him. "And yes, I love you, too, and I want to be your wife."

Epilogue

Nina danced the samba across the floor. Someone had found a disco ball in storage and hung it to illuminate the bar. Nina's parents stood on a makeshift stage at one end of the bar providing the music. Scott tried to copy Nina's moves, but he wasn't quite as limber as she was. She floated on a breeze of happiness. Scott wanted marriage and a family and she did, too. Her love for him filled her as she moved across the dance floor.

The casino was a blaze of light. People laughed and danced and in the background the sound of slot machines chiming added to the festive air.

"Five minutes to midnight," Grace Torres announced in the middle of her song.

People stamped and clapped. Nina found herself too breathless to continue. She grinned at Scott and left him to his sister. Kenzie grabbed him and kept him in the middle of the floor.

Nina took a glass of champagne from a waitress moving through the crowd with a tray.

"This is amazing, Nina, you did it." Miss E. glowed. Jasper hovered over her protectively. "You put the Casa de Mariposa back on the map."

"What's amazing," Nina said, "is your grandson out on the dance floor having fun."

"Miracles happen," Miss E. said. "I thought for sure he'd forgotten how to have fun."

"He was just repressing his fun gene."

Miss E. shook her head. "What he needed was the right woman."

"It's a tough job, but someone had to volunteer," Nina said with a grin.

"Speaking of jobs, I hear you're going to be working for the city of Reno. What happened to Milan and the House of Armani?"

Nina laughed happily. "Who wants Milan when I can have Reno? Besides, Lydia's mom has shown herself so adept at promotion that I decided to hire Caroline and give her the Armani account."

"Who knew?" Miss E. said.

"They wanted old-world elegance and Caroline is perfect for that." Nina was so pleased with the way things were turning out

Scott shook himself loose from Kenzie and moved determinedly toward Nina.

"Two minutes to midnight," Grace yelled into the mic.

Scott grabbed her and kissed her. She cuddled into his embrace. This was where she belonged.

Carl waved at her. He pulled Anastasia along with him onto the dance floor. Nina couldn't keep the happiness she felt for him off her face. Carl and Anastasia had gotten married a couple hours ago. Maybe Nina should go into the matchmaking business, too.

Lydia and Hunter danced past Nina. Kenzie grabbed her brother Donovan and pulled him after her, showing him the dance moves.

Scott pulled her away from the dance floor.

"Is everybody safe?" Nina asked.

"As safe as I can make them."

"Then I think it's time we left the party for our own private celebration."

"One minute to midnight," Grace Torres sang out.

"I like that idea," Scott said.

Slowly the dance floor stilled as people gazed expectantly at Grace.

"Thirty seconds."

As the minute hand wound around the clock people started chanting. "Ten, nine…"

Nina held Scott's hands. The happiness on his face filled her with joy.

"Five…four…three…two…one. Happy New Year!" The crowd roared, stamped their feet and clapped. Somewhere in the casino, someone was winning the ten-million-dollar jackpot.

Nina kissed Scott and then whispered in his ear. "I love you. Let's go make a baby."

* * * * *

The first two stories in the *Love in the Limelight* series, where four unstoppable women find fame, fortune and ultimately... true love.

LOVE IN THE LIMELIGHT

New York Times bestselling author

BRENDA JACKSON

&

A.C. ARTHUR

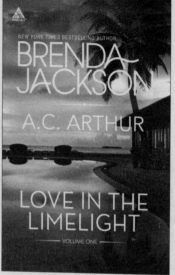

In *Star of His Heart,* Ethan Chambers is Hollywood's most eligible bachelor. But when he meets his costar Rachel Wellesley, he suddenly finds himself thinking twice about staying single.

In *Sing Your Pleasure,* Charlene Quinn has just landed a major contract with L.A.'s hottest record label, working with none other than Akil Hutton. Despite his gruff attitude, she finds herself powerfully attracted to the driven music producer.

Available now wherever books are sold!

www.Harlequin.com

KPLIM1163I014R

REQUEST YOUR FREE BOOKS!

2 FREE NOVELS
PLUS 2 FREE GIFTS!

KIMANI™ ROMANCE

Love's ultimate destination!

YES! Please send me 2 FREE Harlequin® Kimani™ Romance novels and my 2 FREE gifts (gifts are worth about $10). After receiving them, if I don't wish to receive any more books, I can return the shipping statement marked "cancel." If I don't cancel, I will receive 4 brand-new novels every month and be billed just $5.19 per book in the U.S. or $5.74 per book in Canada. That's a savings of at least 20% off the cover price. It's quite a bargain! Shipping and handling is just 50¢ per book in the U.S. and 75¢ per book in Canada.* I understand that accepting the 2 free books and gifts places me under no obligation to buy anything. I can always return a shipment and cancel at any time. Even if I never buy another book, the two free books and gifts are mine to keep forever.

168/368 XDN F4XC

Name _____ (PLEASE PRINT) _____

Address _____ Apt. #

City _____ State/Prov. _____ Zip/Postal Code

Signature (if under 18, a parent or guardian must sign)

Mail to the **Harlequin® Reader Service:**
IN U.S.A.: P.O. Box 1867, Buffalo, NY 14240-1867
IN CANADA: P.O. Box 609, Fort Erie, Ontario L2A 5X3

Want to try two free books from another line?
Call 1-800-873-8635 or visit www.ReaderService.com.

* Terms and prices subject to change without notice. Prices do not include applicable taxes. Sales tax applicable in N.Y. Canadian residents will be charged applicable taxes. Offer not valid in Quebec. This offer is limited to one order per household. Not valid for current subscribers to Harlequin® Kimani™ Romance books. All orders subject to credit approval. Credit or debit balances in a customer's account(s) may be offset by any other outstanding balance owed by or to the customer. Please allow 4 to 6 weeks for delivery. Offer available while quantities last.

Your Privacy—The Harlequin® Reader Service is committed to protecting your privacy. Our Privacy Policy is available online at www.ReaderService.com or upon request from the Harlequin Reader Service.

We make a portion of our mailing list available to reputable third parties that offer products we believe may interest you. If you prefer that we not exchange your name with third parties, or if you wish to clarify or modify your communication preferences, please visit us at www.ReaderService.com/consumerchoice or write to us at Harlequin Reader Service Preference Service, P.O. Box 9062, Buffalo, NY 14269. Include your complete name and address.

KROM13R

Hiring her was a brilliant business move…and a dangerous personal one.

Her Tender Touch

DARA GIRARD

Jason built a software empire from the ground up, but he's missing the one thing that could take his company over the top. Hiring Abby to give him a polished edge with investors is a brilliant business move. Until she unleashes a desire that has Jason aching to show the gorgeous etiquette coach a few maneuvers of his own. With Jason's top secret new product—and both their futures—on the line, is Abby ready to gamble everything on love?

"Girard's writing is inspirational and poetic, with one-liners that will stick with readers long after they reach the final page."
—*RT Book Reviews* on *PERFECT MATCH*

Available December 2014 wherever books are sold!

KPDG3821214